NINE MONTHS

Shawna

by Maggie Wells

E

EPIC
Press

Shawna
Nine Months: Book #5

Written by Maggie Wells

Copyright © 2016 by Abdo Consulting Group, Inc.

Published by EPIC Press™
PO Box 398166
Minneapolis, MN 55439

Printed in the United States of America.

Cover design by Candice Keimig
Images for cover art obtained from iStockPhoto.com
Edited by Lisa Owens

LIBRARY OF CONGRESS CATALOGING-IN-PUBLICATION DATA

Wells, Maggie.
Shawna / Maggie Wells.
p. cm. — (Nine months ; #5)
Summary: Shawna, an 18-year-old living in Oakland, California waits to have sex for
the very first time with her longtime boyfriend, Philippe, but the protection fails and
she becomes pregnant. Philippe wants her to abort the baby but she can't go through
with it. Shawna finds juggling motherhood and college extremely difficult and makes
a mistake that endangers her baby.
ISBN 978-1-68076-194-8 (hardcover)
1. Teenagers—Sexual behavior—Fiction. 2. Teenage pregnancy—Fiction.
3. Sex—Fiction. 4. Abortion—Fiction. 5. Young adult fiction. I. Title.
[Fic]—dc23
2015949414

EPIC
Press

EPICPRESS.COM

To Allison for her inspiration

One

A COLD FOG HAD ROLLED IN FROM THE BAY AND BLAN-KETED OAKLAND. SHAWNA PULLED ON HER FLEECE sweats and stood in front of the mirror to inspect her body. She stared at her reflection. Her eyes rested on her belly. Pulling her top up and turning sideways, she looked for a telltale bump, but it was flat and firm, as usual. She unzipped her hoodie to examine her breasts. They looked the same but they were tender to the touch, as though they were bruised.

Shawna heard the sound of the bathroom door shutting out in the hall—her mother! She flicked the overhead switch and crawled into bed. She reached for the lamp switch on the nightstand and dug under her mattress for her journal. She paged back through the journal to reflect on what she had written each day over the past couple of weeks.

May 4. Weight: 123 (She weighed herself every morning.)

Dear Diary: Met Philippe at Heinold's to play pool and hang with his posse. Sat in his car afterward and made out.

May 9. Weight: 126
Dear Diary: I'm late and I'm afraid to tell Philippe.

Her phone buzzed. It was Philippe.

Where are you? he texted.

Home, she replied.

Come out? he asked. **Meet at Heinold's?**

Give me an hour, she replied.

Shawna watched as Philippe leaned over the pool table, lining up a shot. "Are you going to talk to me?" she asked.

Philippe glanced up from the pool balls, his green eyes meandering up the length of her body before reaching her eyes. She wore her hair up in a high ponytail, the tail of which fanned out over her shoulders. "What's up, baby?" he asked.

He laid down his pool cue and walked over to her. He leaned against her with his lips lightly brushing hers while he ran his hand over her hip and up her back, under her blouse. She leaned into him and the temptation of sensation, that full-body rush. But she pulled back, realizing that this was how she had gotten into this mess in the first place.

"Philippe." Shawna pulled away before he could grab her breasts. She reached for his hand—to keep it off her—and began massaging his palm. Her thumbs dug deep into his flesh. She waited until he looked into her eyes. "We have a problem."

"Really?" he asked.

Shawna could see that he wasn't really listening to her.

"It can wait," he said. "It's been too long." He leaned in to kiss her again.

"No," she said.

"What?" he asked, impatient.

"It's just," she said. "You know I didn't want to go all the way. But you said it was okay."

"What?" he asked, incredulous. He pulled away from her and looked at her, a wary expression on his face.

"It's just that I think I might be pregnant," she said.

Philippe stared at her. She stared back. The desire in his eyes was gone; his eyes were stone cold. "Are you sure?"

"I'm three weeks late," she said.

Philippe turned back to the pool table and lined up his next shot. "Have you taken a test?"

"No," she said.

The cue ball careened off the table onto the floor and everyone turned to stare.

"Shit!" Philippe flung the cue onto the table. "Then take one. Go to the drugstore." He stormed toward the door and then turned on his heel. "And don't tell me this is my fault! You wanted it as much as I did." He spun around and stomped out, slamming the door behind him.

Shawna was stunned. Seriously? "Fuck you, Philippe!" she screamed. They had been going steady since freshman year. Now that they were seniors, she thought they would be together forever—go to college together, get married, have a family. She thought that was his plan too. *But now everything is ruined*, she thought. And he was right; it was all her fault.

//

Shawna sat on the toilet and stared at the stick in her hand. Her own body had betrayed her. How could this be happening? Enormous responsibility weighed heavily on her. *Responsible,* she thought. *I'm responsible for this—for a baby, for this life inside me—responsible for the next eighteen years.*

//

The phone rang five times before he picked up.

"Philippe. It's me, Shawna."

"Uh-huh." His voice was stone cold.

"I took the test."

"Yeah?"

"I am," she said.

For a second she thought he had hung up. Then she heard him mutter, "Shit."

"I know," she said. Tears burned her eyes and slid down her cheeks.

Philippe cleared his throat. "Here's what we are going to do. We'll go to the clinic after school tomorrow and get it confirmed. Those home tests are wrong sometimes, you know."

Shawna knew the test wasn't wrong but she didn't

argue. She was glad that he was taking charge—that he would be by her side. *We are in this together,* she thought.

"Do you want to do something today?" Shawna asked. She really didn't want to be alone to think about it—maybe he would hold her in his arms and show her that he cared about her and what she was feeling.

"Do something?"

"Hang out, go for a walk on the Embarcadero," Shawna said. "Do something."

"I can't," he said.

"Fine." Shawna hung up the phone before he could give her some lame excuse. What could be more important than being with her right now? Her tears of sadness had turned to fury. *How could she have been so stupid?*

//

Shawna logged onto Facebook and typed in *teen pregnancy*. She sifted through dozens of pages until she came across Nine Months. Girls as young as fourteen were posting photos, poetry, and music videos into a stream.

Candy: Watch this inspiring movie about Teen Moms and what they can overcome!

Jasmine: Did you know? Well before a girl even knows she is pregnant, her baby's brain has already begun to grow. By five weeks the cerebral cortex has started to develop, the part that allows all of us to move, dance, run, speak, and sing.

Aleecia: I can feel my baby singing along with me in church.

Izzy: Since I became pregnant, my breasts, rear-end, and even my feet have grown. Is there anything that gets smaller during pregnancy? Answer—your bladder!

Luci: Is anybody here considering abortion?

Shawna: I am. I guess. My boyfriend wants to take me to a clinic.

Shawna sent friend requests to all the girls and then, hearing a noise at the front door, she shut her laptop.

Two

"WHERE ARE WE GOING?" SHAWNA YELLED OVER THE rap song blaring on the car radio.

"West Oakland," Philippe yelled back. "We don't want to run into anyone from school."

Shawna nodded and sat back in her seat. The heater in Philippe's car didn't work so she pulled her sweater tight around her and winced at the soreness in her breasts.

Philippe went back to singing along with the rapper and banging out a rhythm on the steering wheel. She began to think that he had done this before. He seemed so unconcerned. He pulled into a small parking lot and she saw the sign: Planned

Parenthood. Was he taking her here for a test or for an abortion? Both, probably.

The receptionist told Shawna to add her name to the long list on a clipboard and to take a seat. The waiting room was full; the only two vacant chairs were across the room from each other. Philippe flopped down onto one, picked up a Sports Illustrated, and thumbed through it. Shawna sank down onto the remaining chair. On her right, a young black chick coughed—a hard, phlegmy, rattling cough. Shawna turned away just in time to see the small boy on her left hit his baby sister in the face with a toy truck. The baby screamed, the mother smacked the little boy and he let out a howl.

"Shawna Black." She heard her name and approached the front desk.

"I'm Shawna," she said.

"You'll need to fill this out." The receptionist handed Shawna a clipboard with a stack of forms. "I need a photo I.D. and your insurance card," she said.

Shawna returned to her seat and filled in her medical history. She paused at the question "Reason for Today's Visit." This was so humiliating. She thought about the video she had watched on Facebook. A teen mom had said, "I wish health professionals would act like they were here to help us, instead of judging us."

Shawna looked over at Philippe. *Judging,* she thought. Guys aren't judged when their girlfriend gets pregnant. Only the girl is judged. She turned her focus back to the clipboard. She wrote in "pregnancy test" and handed the clipboard back to the receptionist.

After what seemed like forever, her name was called again. She looked over at Philippe, expecting him to join her. But he was engrossed in his magazine and didn't even look at her. She followed the nurse down the hallway, alone.

The nurse drew some blood and left Shawna sitting on the examination table in a flimsy gown to wait for the doctor. The woman who came in after what seemed like an hour didn't look old enough to be a doctor, but she shook Shawna's hand and introduced herself as Dr. Yoon Chun. She looked over the paperwork on the clipboard.

"So you think you might be pregnant?" Dr. Chun asked.

"The EPT was positive," Shawna replied. "And I feel gross. Bloated, my breasts are sore. I read about the symptoms on the Internet."

"You are . . . how old?" Shawna could see her doing the math in her head. "Seventeen?"

"I'm almost eighteen."

The doctor smiled. "So where's the father?" she asked.

"In the waiting room," Shawna said.

"Really?" Dr. Chun asked. "What's he doing out there?"

"I don't know," Shawna said. "Waiting, I guess."

"What's his name?" Dr. Chun asked.

"Philippe," Shawna said.

"Excuse me. I'll be right back." Shawna could

hear the doctor's heels click on the tile floor of the hallway. She returned a few minutes later with a sullen-looking Philippe.

"Have a seat," Dr. Chun said.

Philippe refused to look at Shawna as he slouched in the chair.

"So," Dr. Chun said to Philippe. "Shawna is pregnant."

Philippe looked up. "You already did the test?"

"The lab results won't be back until tomorrow but Shawna is sure and I'm ninety percent certain that she's right," Dr. Chun said. "Have you considered your options?"

"Options?" Philippe sounded incredulous. "I'm eighteen, she's seventeen, so there's nothing to consider. She has to get an abortion."

"Abortion is one choice," Dr. Chun said. "There's also adoption, and parenthood."

Philippe snorted. "Why would you try to talk a seventeen-year-old into having a baby? It can't be good for her or the baby."

"I'm not trying to talk anybody into anything," Dr. Chun said. "But you need to have all the facts to make an informed decision."

Philippe shook his head. "I can't believe this," he said.

"Why weren't you using birth control?" Dr. Chun asked.

"We were!" Philippe exclaimed. "I'm not stupid. We used a condom. And we only did it once."

"It only takes one time," Dr. Chun said. "And I'm sure you know that condoms aren't one hundred percent effective. Nothing is—nothing but abstinence."

Dr. Chun looked at Shawna. "Call me tomorrow to get the results. And don't forget, Shawna. This is your choice. Your feelings matter."

//

Philippe was silent on the ride home. He cranked the radio up to the max again.

Shawna turned down the radio and asked, "What are you thinking?"

"You know what I'm thinking," Philippe said. "You need to get an abortion. There is no other choice. You know that. Why are you being so difficult?"

"I'm not trying to be difficult, but can't we talk about this?" Shawna asked. "You told me that you loved me. You told me that we are going to get married someday."

"Nothing has changed," Philippe said.

"Well, this is *our* baby we're talking about," Shawna said, raising her voice. "Why would you want to kill our baby? We always talked about having kids. This is our kid, our first child. Think about that. How could you live with yourself, knowing that you had forced me to abort our baby? What if it was a boy and we never had another son?"

"Forced you?" Philippe cried. "Why am I the bad guy here? If you decide to get an abortion, that's your choice and I'd support you in that decision. Look, here's the truth—I could never face my father with this news. He would be so ashamed of me—he'd probably throw me out and he wouldn't pay for college. My life would be ruined. Is that what you want? And what about your family? You think they'll be thrilled?" He reached over and cranked up the radio again.

What do I want? Shawna wondered. *I don't want to ruin his life or mine, that's for sure. Would this baby ruin our lives? I don't know his father. Would he really cut Philippe off like that? What about my father? What would he say?*

She reached over and slipped her hand into Philippe's. He looked at her sadly and squeezed her hand.

//

Shawna opened her journal.

May 20. Weight: 128
Dear Diary: I've already gained five pounds
this month. Shit! I've really fucked things up.
For me, for Philippe. I hate myself.

Three

SHAWNA PICKED UP THE PHONE AND BEGAN PUNCHING IN the numbers for the clinic. She stopped before punching the last digit. Her hand was shaking and her pounding heart was wedged in her throat. She couldn't catch her breath. There was no way she could get a word out. She sat on the bed, breathing deeply, and started to feel light-headed. *I'll just lie down for a little bit*, she thought.

Shawna woke up an hour later and checked the time. *Shit! I need to speak to Dr. Chun before she leaves for the day.* She quickly dialed the number and waited while it rang.

"Planned Parenthood," the voice said. "How may I help you?"

Shawna cleared her throat. "This is Shawna Black. I saw Dr. Chun yesterday and I was calling to get my test results."

"Date of birth?" the voice asked.

Shawna recited the numbers.

"Yes," the voice said. "Your results came back. I need to schedule a time for you to speak to the doctor."

"Just tell me!" Shawna cried.

"I can't, dear," the voice said. "Only the doctor can speak with you."

"Ask her to call me?" Shawna asked. "Right away, please?"

"I'll give her the message," the voice said. "What's the best number to reach you?"

Shawna recited her cell number and hung up. She paced back and forth in her bedroom. *Call me, call me—I need to know,* she thought, trying to hang onto any shred of hope. *If the results were negative, wouldn't the receptionist have been able to tell me? Maybe not. Give her the benefit of the doubt.*

Her breasts ached in her too-small bra. She unzipped her too-tight jeans and embraced her flat belly. Was something growing inside of her? Was she just imagining it or she did actually feel different?

The ring tone made her jump. She clicked the green button.

"Hello?"

"Shawna, it's me." She recognized Philippe's voice. She knew why he was calling.

"I'm waiting for the doctor to call," Shawna said. "I thought you were her."

"Call me as soon as you know something," Philippe said.

As soon as she hung up the phone buzzed again.

"May I speak with Shawna?" It was Dr. Chun.

"It's me," Shawna said.

"It's Dr. Chun. I have your results."

"Uh-huh." Shawna held her breath.

"It was positive," Dr. Chun said. "You are pregnant. Can we schedule you . . . "

Shawna felt her stomach heave. "I need to go," she said and ended the call. She ran for the bathroom and retched into the toilet. She lay down on the floor and pressed her face against the cool tile, waiting to see if it was over. She brushed her teeth and washed her face, rubbing her face roughly with the terrycloth towel.

She staggered back to her bedroom and dragged herself onto her bed. She stared at the ceiling for a minute and checked her phone. No messages. She opened her laptop and logged on to Facebook. She clicked on the first link and watched the video that Aleecia had posted.

Aleecia: Here's a fun video: watching a pregnant belly grow! So cute.

Candy: Check out this one: One Week Postpartum Belly

Luci: Are you that girl? The girl that got way too

drunk? The one that is too insecure? The one with the random hook up?

Aleecia: You have no idea how special you are to someone. Stop looking down on yourself. Pick yourself up, ask for help, and move on with your life. YOU CAN DO THIS.

Jasmine: Have you heard of Molly Anne? Her mom was sexually assaulted, and gave her baby up for adoption. That baby graduated from college! Check out her story

Izzy: Always find the positive in EVERY situation. Right now sit down and name one thing positive about your current situation.

Shawna thought about that. *What is the positive here? The only thing I can think of is the plus sign on the EPT test!* She slammed her laptop shut. *Positive, my ass!* She heard her mom banging pots and cupboard doors in the kitchen and went to see if she could help.

///

Shawna's stomach lurched as she entered the kitchen. The smell of cooking meat was nauseating; the thought of eating it was even worse.

"Hi, hon. How was your day?" Her mom looked up from chopping vegetables.

"Fine," Shawna said.

"Could you help with the salad?"

"What are you making?" Shawna asked.

"Beef stew," her mom said. "Your favorite."

I don't think I'll ever eat beef stew again, Shawna thought. She rifled through the fridge for things to make a salad. She pulled the lettuce and vegetables from the crisper and reached for the salad dressing when she spotted a jar of pickles. She placed the salad fixings on the counter and went back to the fridge to pull out the pickles. She took a fork and stabbed a pickle, popping it into her mouth. Then she speared another one.

"How was your Calculus test?" her mom asked, glancing up from her chopping.

"I think I did okay." Shawna said. She stabbed another pickle.

Shawna continued eating pickles, unaware that her mom had stopped chopping and was watching her.

"Shawna, the last time I ate so many pickles was when I was pregnant with you."

Shawna's fork froze, mid-stab. Shawna smiled weakly and put the fork down on the counter. She expected her mom to say something else, something accusatory, but she had gone back to chopping vegetables.

//

Philippe met Shawna at her locker before her first class the next day. He touched the back of her arm, tentatively. "Are we okay?" he asked.

She turned to face him. "What are we going to do?" she asked.

"Get an abortion, right?" he asked. "Isn't that what you want to do?"

"Will you come with me?" she asked.

"Of course," he said.

"But we're still going to get married, right?" Shawna said. "Some day?"

"We are," he responded. "Someday. I just don't want to fuck everything up before we can even get started."

//

May 22. Weight: 130

Dear Diary: Philippe said we're going to get married. Some day far in the future—after this baby is dead and gone and forgotten. Will I ever forget this? Will I still want to marry him?

Four

SHAWNA AND PHILIPPE SAT IN MS. JORDAN'S OFFICE. Ms. Jordan was the counselor at Planned Parenthood. She was a large black woman with a booming, jovial presence. Her braided up-do was graying at the temples and she wore dangly earrings and a low-cut knit dress that clung to her generous curves. A dozen bracelets jangled on her arm whenever she moved. Shawna liked her immediately.

She smiled at Shawna. "You're here because you're pregnant and you want to discuss your options?"

Philippe interrupted. "We're here to book an

appointment for an abortion. I don't know why we couldn't do that by phone."

"Is that right, Shawna?" Ms. Jordan asked. "Terminating your pregnancy is not your only choice, Shawna."

"I know that," Shawna said.

"Can you tell me why you think that is the best option for you?" Ms. Jordan asked.

Philippe interrupted again. "Because she's only seventeen."

Ms. Jordan fixed her gaze on Philippe. "Many girls choose to put their babies up for adoption. There are a lot of loving families who can't have children who would be able to give your baby a loving home. And plenty of other girls choose to keep their babies."

"Well, that's just stupid," Philippe said. "Shawna wants to get an abortion and get this over with."

"It's interesting that you're here today, Philippe," Ms. Jordan said. "A lot of girls come alone, or with their mom. You obviously care a lot about Shawna and want what is best for her."

Shawna thought about that. *What is best for me? Why can't I decide? Do the other girls just know what to do, without a second thought?*

"Shawna," Ms. Jordan said. "We need to hear from you. What do you want to do? Before you got pregnant, how did you feel about abortion?"

Shawna considered the question. "Well, first of all, I never thought I'd be faced with it. And I believe that every woman should be able to decide for herself. I would never stand in someone's way and argue that they couldn't have an abortion."

Ms. Jordan nodded. "And Philippe says you've chosen abortion for yourself. Why do you feel that it's the best choice for you?"

Shawna glanced over at Philippe. He was staring at her. "I guess it's like Philippe says. I'm too young."

"Lots of moms have their first child before they are twenty," Ms. Jordan said.

"But, I want to go to college," Shawna said.

"And you can," Ms. Jordan said.

"But it would be way harder, financially and everything," Shawna said.

"Yes, that's true," Ms. Jordan said. "You've obviously thought this through. But is that the only reason?"

"I don't want to disappoint my parents," Shawna said.

"You haven't told them?" Ms. Jordan asked.

"No," Shawna said.

Ms. Jordan nodded sympathetically. "I see. So you feel adoption isn't an option?"

"It would be way too hard to give up a baby," Shawna said. "I can't even imagine."

"Anything else?" Ms. Jordan probed.

Shawna looked at Philippe. "And when I do have a baby someday, I want to have it with someone who loves me."

Philippe stared at her, wide-eyed. "What?" he asked, incredulous. "You know I love you. Why would you say something like that?"

Ms. Jordan looked at Shawna. "Shawna?"

"I think if you loved me, if you really loved me," Shawna said. "You would want to keep our baby."

Philippe scowled and looked down at his lap.

//

"So you've met with the counselor, you've read the literature, and you've made your decision to go through with the procedure?" Dr. Jamali asked. He was a wiry, dark-skinned man. Pakistani, she guessed.

Shawna nodded.

He flipped through papers on his clipboard and without looking up at her, said, "You've signed the consent form. That's it, then." The doctor stood up. "Shawna, a nurse will be in shortly to get you and I'll see you in the treatment room."

A nurse entered the room and handed her a gown. "Everything off from the waist down. Opening in the back. Take a chair outside when you're undressed."

Shawna gingerly took the gown, wondering who had worn it last. Another teenager, sick with remorse? She slipped it on and fumbled with the ties that were too short and positioned in all the wrong places. *Who designs these things,* she wondered, pulling the edges of the thin material tight around herself against the chill of the air conditioning. She might as well have been wearing nothing at all, for all the warmth it gave. She found a chair in the hallway and sat down, clutching the flimsy gown to cover her ass. She picked up a magazine and flipped through it, unable to focus on any of the celebrity photos.

She thought back to yesterday when she'd called Philippe and told him that she didn't want him to go to the clinic with her.

"Who is going with you?" he'd asked. She was sure she'd heard relief in his voice and for a moment she had regretted her decision. *Maybe I shouldn't have let him off the hook so easily. I should have insisted he sit in the lobby and wait. It wouldn't compare to what I have to go through, but it would have been something.*

"My mom," she had lied.

The receptionist had totally bought her story that her mom was parking the car and would be in before the procedure was over. And here she was shivering in her paper gown, aware that she'd have to make up some other story to check herself out of this place.

"Are you okay, dear?" A nurse stood before her, frowning.

"I guess," Shawna said.

"You're holding your stomach," the nurse said. "Are you feeling ill?"

Shawna looked down and noticed that her hands were cupping her belly, protectively. *I've been doing that a lot lately.*

"No," Shawna said. She moved her hands. "I'm all right." But that was just another lie.

"Then follow me," the nurse said. "It's time."

Shawna wondered if her legs could carry her to the treatment room. She suddenly felt queasy.

She followed the nurse into a large, cold room with an examining table in the center, surrounded on both sides by carts piled with surgical supplies. The doctor stood on the far side of the room, pulling on latex gloves.

"Hop up and put your feet in the stirrups," the nurse said.

Shawna did as she was told and stared at the ceiling tiles. Her hands gripped the metal rails of the table and she was shaking uncontrollably. She had never felt so alone and she actually felt like she was going to die. Suddenly she wished she had brought her mother with her.

Five

THE NURSE DRAPED A SHEET OVER HER AND VELCRO-ED a blood-pressure band around her left arm. Shawna winced as the band squeezed her arm in its vise and then released. The nurse jotted something on her clipboard and pushed a thermometer into Shawna's mouth. She held Shawna's wrist, felt the pulse, and studied her watch. She jotted something down again and yanked the thermometer out from Shawna's clenched teeth. Then with the ease that came from years of practice, she slid a thin needle into the skin on the back of Shawna's hand and strung the tubing up to a pole above her head.

"We'll give you a little something to relax you," the nurse said.

The doctor suddenly appeared next to Shawna's head.

"Everything okay?" he asked, his voiced muffled by his surgical mask.

Shawna stared up at him. *Here I am, lying on a cold, hard table with my feet in stirrups, waiting for you to scrape out my insides and you are asking me if I'm okay? Are you joking?*

A little groan escaped from her, but he must have taken that for an affirmative because she heard him roll up the stool at the foot of her cot and then she felt the gown being lifted and her knees being pressed apart. She heard the rattle of cellophane and the clank of metal.

"First, I'm going to insert the speculum," he said. "It's cold but it won't hurt."

It won't hurt, Shawna thought. *Not yet. But soon, I fear.* She had been told to expect some discomfort, some cramping. But what would her baby be feeling as it was being scraped off the side of her uterus? She imagined what her baby would look like, a cross between Philippe's exotic Haitian features and her own copper hue—a hint of her father's Shoshone heritage. As she felt the cold steel instrument enter her, she abruptly made up her mind.

"Stop," she said, struggling to sit up. The nurse placed a hand on her shoulder, but the doctor had already removed the speculum.

"What's the matter?" the doctor asked, looking alarmed, or angry, or both. "Are you in pain?"

"Let me go," Shawna said to the nurse. The doctor nodded and the nurse released the pressure on Shawna's shoulder. Shawna sat up and pulled the gown down over her legs. "I've changed my mind. I can't do this."

"Shawna," the doctor said in a low, calm voice. "You're just a little nervous. That's perfectly normal. Why don't we give you a little something to relax you?"

"No." Shawn shook her head. "I've changed

my mind. You can't force me." Shawna started to stand up and the needle tugged at the skin on her hand.

"Sit down," the nurse snapped. "You'll rip the catheter out. You've already had your consultation and gave consent. You've already booked Dr. Jamali's time. We can't refund your money."

"I don't care about the money!" Shawna screamed. Why was she being so bitchy? Shawna tore at the tubing which caused her hand to bleed. She held her bleeding hand to her mouth. The rusty taste of blood filled her mouth and coated her gums. *I wonder if my baby is able taste things?* The thought made her tear up. "I need to go."

Shawna looked at the doctor and the nurse in the eyes. Then she took a deep breath and lowered her voice. She wanted to sound calm and rational. "I understand that abortion is the right choice for a lot of people," she said. "But it's not the right choice for me. I'm sorry I wasted your time. I want to go home now."

The doctor pushed his stool away from the table. "Take the IV out," he said.

The nurse peeled the tape off of Shawna's hand and removed the IV. Shawna climbed off the table and, clutching her gown to cover her butt, left the room, changed into her clothes, and walked out of the clinic.

//

When she got home, Shawna texted Philippe.

I need to talk to you.

What's up?

In person.

Heinold's?

okay

//

Philippe was sitting in a booth drinking a Red Bull when Shawna walked into the pub. Shawna sat down opposite him and reached her hands across the table. He took her hand in his and squeezed it.

"Was it awful?" he asked. "I should have been there with you."

"I changed my mind." Her voice came out as a croak.

"What?" Philippe exclaimed. "You didn't go?"

Shawna looked at him and tried to decide if his expression was angry or elated. "No, I was at the clinic. The doctor was about to begin and then . . . " She covered her face with her hands. "Oh my God, it was horrible!"

Philippe didn't say anything. His eyes bore into her as though trying to read her soul.

"I suddenly realized that I couldn't kill my baby," Shawna said.

"Our baby," Philippe said. He reached across the table and took both of her hands in his.

Shawna stared at Philippe as if she were seeing him for the first time. *Is he really going to do this?*

she thought. *Are we going to get married and have this baby together?*

"I've been thinking about it," he said. "I was a real shit the other day, at the clinic."

"Yeah, you were," Shawna said.

"Well, that's not who I am," Philippe said. "I'm not going to let you to through this alone. I'll go with you the next time."

Shawna pulled her hands away and slammed her palm on the table. "You're not listening to me," she cried. "I'm not going back there. I'm going to have this baby. I'm going to tell everyone—my parents, my friends . . . everyone. I'm going to get big and fat, and then go into labor, give birth—the whole nine yards. I'm doing this thing. That's my decision." She paused, and looked right into his eyes. "So, are you in or what?"

"In for what?" Phillipe answered. "For keeping the baby? What about college? What about our plans?"

"I don't know," Shawna said, sadly. "We have

seven months to figure that part out. I just mean are you still my boyfriend? Will you be with me through all of this?"

"This is really going to mess up your life," Philippe said. "Both of our lives."

"Look," Shawna said. "I'm doing it with or without you. But I'd rather you be involved. Like you said, it's our baby. What happens next, we can decide together."

Philippe looked at Shawna for a long time. He seemed to be considering his options. Shawna started to panic, thinking he might actually say that he was washing his hands of her. Finally he said, "I love you, Shawna. I don't think this is the right decision. I really don't. But of course—if you're in, I'm all in too."

//

She couldn't wait to get home to tell the girls on Facebook.

Shawna: I'm having my baby. And Philippe said he's all in!

Aleecia: God is smiling down on you today.

Jasmine: I just read this quote: "The positive thinker sees the invisible, feels the intangible, and achieves the impossible."

Candy: Here's one: "Stop worrying about what you have to lose and focus on what you have to gain."

Izzy: I lost my husband in Afghanistan. No matter how good or bad you think your life is, wake up each day and be thankful for life. Someone, somewhere in the world is fighting for their life.

///

May 29. Weight 134
Dear Diary, I'm having my baby! Our baby.
I'm not ready to tell Mom and Dad. Not yet.

Six

SHAWNA STARTED GETTING SICK EVERY DAY BETWEEN second and third periods. She had to ask for a pass and then would go lie down in the nurse's office. After the third time, the nurse became suspicious.

"This isn't the flu, is it?" Nurse Bailey asked.

"I don't know," Shawna said. She had wanted to put off this conversation as long as possible.

"Have you seen a doctor?" Nurse Bailey asked.

"Yes," Shawna said.

"You're pregnant?" Nurse Bailey asked.

"Yes," Shawna said.

"How far along are you?" Nurse Bailey asked.

Shawna did the math in her head. "Three months," she replied.

"What's your plan?" Nurse Bailey asked.

"I'm not getting an abortion, if that's what you mean," Shawna said.

"Okay. We'll need to enroll you in the teen mom program. They will help you make up work that you miss due to sickness or other complications. Have you told your parents?"

"I need to wait," Shawna said. "They'll want me to get an abortion. I need to wait until it's too late."

"Some abortions are done much later than twelve weeks," Nurse Bailey said. "How long can you possibly wait? Why are you afraid to tell them?"

"It's not that I'm afraid," Shawna said. "It's just that they're going to be so shocked—and disappointed. I have been their good girl my whole life."

"Clearly, you've thought a lot about this," Nurse Bailey said. "Well, we can't enroll you in the teen mom program without parental consent. You are putting me in an awkward position. Surely you don't want them to find out via a letter from the school?"

"No," Shawna said, slowly. "My mom would never forgive me."

"Would you like me to be with you when you tell your parents?" Nurse Bailey asked.

Shawna hesitated, considering the offer. Nurse Bailey's presence would ensure that the conversation would be calm and rational, clinical actually. But awkward—really awkward. She shook her head. "Thanks. That's okay," she said. "I can do it."

"So then what?" Nurse Bailey asked. "They will want to know what you're going to do with the baby."

"I know," Shawna said.

"Have you considered adoption?" Nurse Bailey asked.

"I don't know," Shawna said. "I figured I had a few months to think about it."

Nurse Bailey retrieved her purse from her desk drawer. "This is a bit out of my purview," she said. "But I moonlight as a social worker with an adoption agency." She dug a brochure out of her purse. "I could connect you with them. They help you choose a couple that shares your values, someone who would raise your child the way you would want. You can interview as many couples as you like, until you find the right one."

Shawna stared at her hands and nodded.

"There are many childless couples who would do anything to adopt a baby," Nurse Bailey continued.

Who's to say I don't want this baby? Shawna thought. Then she took the brochure and thumbed through it anyway.

"Babies need two parents, Shawna," Nurse Bailey said. "And not just for conception. Babies are a lot of work."

"Lots of kids are raised by single parents," Shawna argued.

"That's true," Nurse Bailey said. "And a lot of single parents raise well-adjusted kids. But it is extra hard."

Shawna was no longer listening.

//

When Shawna got home, she was surprised to see her mom's car in the driveway. Her mother was a professor at Berkeley and usually didn't get home until after six o'clock. Shawna snuck in through the back door and went straight to her room. *No putting it off,* she thought. *Tonight is the night.*

Dinner was unusually quiet that night. Normally her dad would go on and on about his day. He was a criminal defense attorney and regaled them at dinner with the dramatic exploits of his clients. Shawna worried that they already knew or suspected something but were afraid to broach the topic.

Finally her mother broke the tension. "How are

you feeling, honey?" her mom asked in a deliberately casual voice. But Shawna noticed she was tapping her foot agitatedly on floor. "Is everything okay?"

Shawna knew then that Nurse Bailey had called her mom. Her father put down his fork and looked expectantly at her.

Shawna took a deep breath. *This is it.* She felt her face burning. "I'm pregnant."

Her father's face took on an unnatural crimson hue and her mom set her silverware gently down on her plate.

"You're sure?" her father asked.

"Yes, I've been tested." Shawna kept her eyes fixed to her plate and pushed the broccoli and potatoes around her plate with her fork.

"I didn't know you were sexually active," her mom said.

Shawna rolled her eyes. *Sexually active makes me sound like I am some kind of slut, doing it all the time with every boy in school.* "I'm not, Mom.

Philippe and I did it one time, I swear. We used birth control and everything. One time, that's it."

Her parents stared at her in silence.

"I found out a couple of weeks ago," Shawna continued speaking in order to break the awkward silence. "I went to an abortion clinic but I changed my mind."

"Changed your mind?" her father asked.

"Yeah," Shawna said. "Changed my mind. Decided I couldn't do it."

"Why?" he asked.

"Because," Shawna said.

Her father glared at her.

"Because it didn't feel right," she said.

"So you're not going to get an abortion?" her mother asked.

"No," Shawna said. "Are you paying attention? I'm not going to get an abortion."

"What about Philippe?" her mother asked. "Does he know?"

"Yes, he knows that I'm pregnant and he knows

that I'm having the baby," Shawna said. She was becoming weary of all the questions. "Are we done now?"

"You told the school nurse before you told me?" her mother asked. "I'm sorry, honey, the school nurse called today. She said it was her duty to inform us."

"Look, I've been in her office every morning, barfing and resting," Shawna said. "She guessed; I didn't tell her. I'm sorry you had to hear it from her. She said I needed your signature to enter the teen mom program at school. I figured she would tell you but I was hoping to tell you first."

"Why did you wait so long to tell us?" her father asked.

"I figured if I had the abortion you would never have had to find out and I could still be your good little girl," Shawna said.

"Oh, sweetie." Her mother dabbed her eyes with her napkin.

Seven

"SO WHAT'S THE PLAN NOW?" HER FATHER ASKED. "You're seventeen years old and you're going to have a baby?"

"That's kind of how it works, Dad," Shawna said and immediately regretted her tone. "I'm sorry, Daddy, I don't mean to sound snarky. This has been a really stressful month. Look, I've thought about it. I know this will be really embarrassing for you, for the whole family. If you'd like me to go away somewhere until after the baby comes . . . ?"

"Go away?" Her father frowned and rubbed the stubble on his chin. "What do you mean?"

"I don't know," Shawna said. "What about Aunt Amy? Would she let me stay with her?"

"Probably," he said. "But we don't want you to go away. We're not ashamed of you."

Shawna looked at her mom. Her eyes were closed and her hands were clasped in her lap as if she were lost in prayer.

"Mom?" Shawna said.

Shawna's mom opened her eyes and asked, "So what happens after the baby is born?"

Shawna shook her head. "I don't know," she said. "Nurse Bailey works with an adoption agency. If I want, I can choose the couple."

"What do you mean, if you want?" Her father stood up and started pacing. "Are you thinking of keeping the baby? What about college? What about your future?"

"It must be hard for the couples who get interviewed but aren't chosen," Shawna's mom said. "They would get their hopes up, I guess."

"Can't we decide this later?" Shawna asked. "We have six months to think about it."

"No," her mother said decisively, surprising all of them. "You're not going to give away my grandchild. I couldn't live with that. I'll raise the baby." She looked at her husband, fiercely. "Shawna will go to college and we'll take care of the baby."

"What?" Shawna's dad exclaimed. "Where did that idea come from? Are you crazy?"

"Charlie," she said. "I really want to be a grandmother. I'm ready to be a grandmother. This is our flesh and blood, our grandchild."

//

Shawna lay on her bed, staring at the ceiling. She was in complete shock. Her mom wanted to raise her baby. She had heard about this happening but couldn't imagine that it was happening to her. She had read in *US Weekly* that Jack Nicholson found out late in life that the woman he called Mom was actually his grandmother and the woman he thought was his sister was actually his mother. *Is that what we're doing?* she wondered. *Is my baby going to grow up thinking I'm his sister?* And when he found out the truth, would he be damaged for life? Or worse, would he believe that his grandmother raised him because his mom was some loser tramp?

Not that there isn't an upside here, she thought. Her baby would be raised in comfort and security while she went to college, and he/she wouldn't be raised by strangers. As Nurse Bailey had said, he/she would be raised by a couple who shared her values, someone who would raise her child the way she had been raised. She could see her/him whenever she wanted. *Once I am on my feet and financially secure, my baby could come live with me. Perfect! But what about that bonding thing,* she wondered. Would her baby bond with her mother? *Would he/she treat me like some creepy aunt?* That would be unbearable. She thought about Jack Nicholson again and how traumatized he had been by the whole thing. What if she told her mother no? *No, you're not raising my baby!*

//

Shawna walked into the kitchen where her mom was slicing carrots. On weekends, her mom always cooked elaborate meals to make up for the take-out Shawna and her dad ordered during the week.

"Mom?" Shawna ventured.

"Yes, dear," her mom said.

"So, how exactly will this work?" Shawna asked.

"I've already come up with names," her mother said, excitedly. "If it's a girl, we'll name her Genevieve. If it's a boy, I like Sawyer."

"Seriously?" Shawna said. "I *hate* those names! Philippe is Haitian and we're Shoshone. What's with the WASP-y names?"

"Genevieve isn't WASP-y," her mom protested. "It's French. When you were two, we had an au

pair from France named Genevieve." She pro-
nounced it Gen-Vi-Ev.

"Okay." Shawna said. "Let's just pretend that
the intention was to make the baby's name sound
Haitian. Shouldn't we consult Philippe's family?"

Shawna's mother stood still and stared out of
the kitchen window.

"Mom?" Shawna said. "What about Philippe?
Shouldn't he be involved in these decisions?"

"You know," her mom's voice sounded as
if she were speaking from a million miles away.
"We always wanted a second child. Don't get me
wrong, Shawna, we loved you, I mean we love
you, to death. You are so precious to us. But we
tried hard to have a second child, maybe a boy.
You could have had a little brother. But I miscarried. Twice. And the third one—we named him
Richard. Richard was born premature and lived for
almost twenty-four hours. I held him in my arms
as he gasped his last breath."

"Oh, Mom!" Shawna cried as she ran to her

mother and embraced her in a bear hug. "I never knew that. I'm so sorry."

"I think when you broke your news to us, your dad and I, well, it took us back to a painful time. We tried so hard to save him, little Richard—Richard the lion-hearted. We named him that because he fought so hard to survive. I've wanted so badly, for so long, to hold a little baby in my arms. And now you've brought us this most amazing gift, Shawna."

"But Mom," Shawna said. "What about Philippe? What about his mom? What do we do?"

"As always," her mom said. "You are right. You are my precious, beautiful child who knows the right thing to say at all the right times. Shawna, I am so proud of you, I want you to know that."

Proud. Shawna blanched at the word. The one thing she never expected her parents to feel about this situation was pride. This was absolutely unexpected—and totally bizarre. She felt things slipping away—out of her control. This whole thing had become more about them than about her.

"So, what do you think?" Shawna asked. "Should we invite Philippe and his mom over to talk?"

"That would be best, wouldn't it?" her mom said. "What about brunch tomorrow? Daddy could grill something—maybe some salmon. Do they like salmon?"

"Mom, I have no idea!" Shawna said. "Why not something simpler? Like burgers or chicken salad?"

"Is she going to fight me on this?" Shawna's mom asked.

Shawna was floored. What was happening here? "Um, Mom? Fight you? What are we fighting about?"

"Our baby," her mom said.

Shawna felt bile rise in her throat and a strange tightness in her chest. What was this feeling? Jealousy? Panic? She felt herself losing control of her body, her choices, her life. Her mom couldn't just take her baby away, could she?

Eight

ER MOM TURNED TO LOOK AT SHAWNA. SHE HAD A weird, faraway look in her eyes. "I'm glad you chose not to have an abortion," she said at last.

Shawna looked at her mom, surprised. "Really?"

Her mom nodded, looking down at the floor. "I didn't want to say anything in front of your dad. There's something he doesn't know."

Shawna sat down on a kitchen stool and studied her mom's face.

"My parents never went to college," her mom said. "And my dream was to get a PhD and become a professor."

"And you did," Shawna said.

"But I almost didn't," her mom said.

"Why not?" Shawna asked.

"Because I got pregnant when I was seventeen," her mom said. "Just like you."

Shawna's eyes grew wide. "Dad doesn't know about this?"

Shawna's mom twisted her wedding band around on her finger as she spoke. "When I told my boyfriend, he thought we should get married right away. He was working as a security guard and studying criminal justice. I knew that if I married him and had the baby I would never be able to leave Fresno. But not marrying him wasn't an option either. I never told him this—but my girlfriend drove me to San Francisco and I got an abortion. I told my boyfriend that I had miscarried. I didn't tell my parents or anyone else. It was awful and I had nightmares for years about it. I think about that baby every day of my life. I never told your dad about it but I have always wondered if that abortion was the reason I had so many miscarriages. If that was the reason that baby Richard died."

Shawna spoke softly. "But you made it out of Fresno and you met Dad and you had me. So aren't you glad you did what you did?"

Shawna's mom nodded but she looked as if she were about to cry. "Yes, I have the life I had always dreamed of. But I find it so strange that you've followed in my footsteps this way. I can't help but think it's not a coincidence. God brought this baby to us. Maybe he's giving me a second chance to get it right this time."

"You know that it's my baby, right?" Shawna asked. *Is my mom delusional?* she wondered. "Mine and Philippe's? I appreciate your offer to help me raise the baby, to let me go to college and all. But the baby will know that you're his grandmother, right? It will know that I'm his mom."

"Of course, sweetheart," Shawna's mom said, dabbing at her eyes. "Where I grew up, mothers lived with their daughters and helped with the babies. It's only natural. It takes a village, right?"

Shawna felt terrible for doubting her mother's intentions. She stood and walked toward her mom to give her a hug.

"Call Philippe," her mom said. The coldness in her tone stopped Shawna in her tracks. "Do his parents know?" she asked.

"I don't know," Shawna said. "I don't think so."

"Well, let's get this over with," her mom said. "Invite them over for lunch. Chicken salad—good idea."

//

Shawna answered the doorbell to find Philippe and his parents standing there, looking uncomfortable.

"Hi, Mr. and Mrs. Henri," Shawna said. "Please come in. My mom is setting up the picnic table out back."

Shawna escorted Philippe's parents to the

backyard and then grabbed him by the arm. "Come inside," she whispered.

Philippe followed her back inside the house and into the bathroom where she locked the door.

"What do your parents know?" Shawna asked.

"Nothing," he said. "I was hoping you would change your mind and I wouldn't have to tell them anything."

"Why do they think we invited them over?" Shawna asked.

"They don't have a clue," he said. "But let's just say they are suspicious that it isn't going to be good news."

"Well, here's a news flash for you," Shawna said. "My mom doesn't want me to have an abortion. She has decided that she's going to raise the baby so that I can go to college. Do you think that's weird? What will your mom think?"

"Jesus!" Philippe said. "What the hell is happening? What about what I think? Don't I have some say in all of this? I'm not ready to be a father. And I'm pretty sure my mom feels the same way."

Shawna recoiled. *It may take a village*, she thought, *but the villagers are about to revolt.* "We'd better get out there," she said.

//

"Here they are," her mom said in a singsong voice as Shawna and Philippe stepped out the back door and onto the patio. "Kids, grab a sandwich and come sit."

Jesus, Shawna thought. Her mom was acting like it was some kind of garden party when in reality World War III was about to break out.

When everyone was seated, Shawna's mom spoke. "Gaby, David, we have some news." Shawna didn't even know that her mom knew Philippe's parents' names. This was all becoming surreal. "Shawna, why don't you start?"

Shawna looked at Philippe in a panic and then stammered. "Um, I'm pregnant."

Mrs. Henri looked like she was going to have a stroke. "And?" she asked. "Are we to assume that Philippe is the father? Do we need a paternity test?"

"No, Mom," Philippe said. "We don't need a paternity test. Geez."

Mrs. Henri regained her composure. "Thank you for telling us. I can't say that I am shocked. The lunch invitation was kind of a giveaway. I've been close to hyperventilating all the way over here." She moved around uncomfortably, and then finally leaned forward in her seat. "I apologize for my son's irresponsible behavior. We are happy to pay for the procedure."

Shawna was shaking now. She never expected to have to face Philippe's mother. "I'm not getting an abortion," she mumbled.

"What?" Mrs. Henri asked. "You are going to ruin your life? My son's life? Is that what you want? Is this some kind of revenge?" She glared at Shawna's mother. "Is this how you raised your daughter? Did you know that she was sexually active?"

That phrase again, Shawna thought. "I'm *not*!" she screamed. "Philippe and I have been together since freshman year and we only did it once. We're not active!"

"Gaby, please," Shawna's mom said. "We're supporting Shawna's decision. She considered abortion and decided that it wasn't right for her."

"My son isn't ready to be a father," Mrs. Henri said. "He's going to college. He has plans for his future. You can't make this decision for him."

"Philippe doesn't need to change his plans," Shawna's mom said. "I'm going to raise the baby so both of the kids can go to college and start their careers."

"You're what?" Mrs. Henri screamed. "Philippe has rights, we have rights." She looked at her husband. "Why haven't you said anything?"

"Um," Mr. Henri said. "How does this work exactly? Are we supposed to pay some kind of child support? What if Philippe wants custody? What if we want visitation rights? This is our grandchild we're talking about. Who will pay for the child's education?"

"Charlie is an attorney," Shawna's mom said. "Charlie, what do you think?"

"David," Shawna's dad said, looking right at Phillipe's father. "This would not be my first choice either. Shawna has made her decision and for some reason that I can't fathom, her mother is supporting her in this. I'm sure we can draft an agreement on custody, visitation, and support that is mutually agreeable to all parties. Philippe can have as much or as little involvement as he desires. The same applies to you and Gaby."

Nine

"SHAWNA MADE A DECISION?" MRS. HENRI SCREAMED. "Philippe, did you make a decision?"

"I wanted Shawna to get an abortion," Philippe said. "I thought she wanted it too. I drove her to the clinic."

"I'm sorry," Shawna said. "I couldn't go through with it."

"So, what exactly is your plan?" Mrs. Henri said, looking at Philippe and then back to Shawna. Her voice had turned cold. "Shotgun wedding? Forgo college, and get minimum wage jobs, rob yourselves of any future?"

"We didn't have a plan," Shawna said. "And I

wasn't asking Philippe for anything. I didn't know my mom would offer to help."

"What makes you think we're going to give up our rights?" Mr. Henri said. "We can't control your decision to have this child but what if we want custody? If Shawna doesn't want to raise the child maybe Gaby does? Our customs are very different from yours."

"I never said I didn't want to raise my child," Shawna said. *How did this get so fucked up,* she wondered. *Everyone is fighting over my baby!*

"Shawna is not giving up custody," Charlie said after seeing Shawna's face turn ghost-white. "That's never been on the table. I think what Vivian meant to say is that she will babysit while Shawna is in class. I'm sure Gaby would love to babysit as well, am I right?"

"Vivian, you're a tenured professor, correct?" Mr. Henri asked. "Are you planning to quit your job to stay home with the baby?"

"I really did not see this conversation going in

this direction," Shawna's mom said. "We only just learned about the pregnancy. We haven't thought through all of the logistics. There's time for that. The baby isn't due for six months. The point is, we are looking at this as a blessing."

"Where *did* you see this conversation going?" Mrs. Henri asked.

"I know it's shocking news," Vivian said. "This baby is going to change all of our lives forever. It's a big decision—Charlie and I understand that. But I thought you'd be happy to know that we are stepping up to support Shawna, and Philippe, too, if he wants to be involved. The child will want for nothing. The kids will finish college and maybe one day they will choose to marry. But they will be able to avoid any hardship that this pregnancy may have caused. We thought you'd be happy about that," she said again.

Philippe's parents rose to leave. "Draft your proposal and send it over," Mr. Henri said. "I'll have my attorney review it. I assume you're covering our legal fees?"

Charlie scowled and looked at his wife through narrowed eyes. "Sure," he muttered.

"Well, it was lovely to meet you," Shawna's mom said in that weird singsong voice again. "I'm sorry it couldn't have been under better circumstances. I hope we can figure this all out—together."

"I'm sure we'll be seeing a lot of each other from now on," Mrs. Henri said without smiling. "Philippe, let's go."

//

Shawna stood in the doorway and watched them drive off. Philippe was sitting in the back seat slumped over. Mrs. Henri was screaming something that Shawna couldn't hear.

Shawna's mom walked up behind her. "Well, that didn't go as well as I would have hoped," she said.

"You think?" Shawna muttered and stomped upstairs to her room.

Shawna logged onto Facebook to see what the girls were up to.

Jasmine: Someone is fighting every day to live. How do you spend your days?

Shawna: I'm keeping my baby. My mom wants to raise it. Is that weird?

Luci: You saw the US Weekly thing about how Jack Nicholson was raised by his grandmother?

Izzy: I know, right? And look how fucked up he turned out to be.

Aleecia: When my boyfriend and I found out we had no idea what to do, and of course the first thing that comes to mind is abortion. My mom helps out too. I think it's normal.

Candy: My mom is a total bitch. I have to pay the housekeeper to help out.

Shawna: My boyfriend's parents are pissed. I think they would rather have the baby murdered.

Candy: My baby daddy's parents feel the same

way. They wish me and the baby would dry up and blow away.

///

June 15. Weight 135

Dear Diary: We told the parents. Now everyone knows. Philippe's dad is pissed! My parents are fighting. I can hear them in the kitchen. I'm ruining everything! What if my parents get divorced? Will Mom still be here to help me?

Shawna texted Philippe: Call me. Within minutes, her phone buzzed. She picked up.

"Hey," Shawna said. "What was your mom saying to you in the car?"

"You don't want to know," Philippe said. "She said a lot of really nasty things."

"About me?" Shawna asked.

"Like I said, you don't want to know."

"But your parents know that we're doing this together, right?" Shawna asked.

"Seems like it." Philippe sounded depressed.

"Did your dad say anything about not paying for college?" Shawna asked.

"A lot of things were said," Philippe responded. "Let's give them some time and let everyone cool off, okay?"

"My parents are fighting too," Shawna said. "Everybody is mad at me. I feel like the whole world is against us."

"I know," Philippe said. "Are you really sure? Have you really made up your mind?"

"Yes." Shawna said. "And it's final. I need your support on this. It's hard enough as it is!"

//

Shawna had taken to hanging out in Nurse Bailey's office between periods regardless of whether she felt nauseated.

"Are you really sure about this?" Nurse Bailey asked at school the next day. "Is there any chance you could change your mind? You could still get an abortion. It's still legal in California up to twenty-four weeks."

"How is that even possible?" Shawna asked.

"You would have to get a Dilation and Evacuation abortion," Nurse Bailey said. "It's a surgical procedure and it usually takes about thirty minutes. The day before they would give you some meds to soften your cervix and then you go back the next day to have the fetus removed."

"That sounds so horrible!" Shawna exclaimed. "And the baby comes out in pieces, right?"

"I guess you've read about the Planned Parenthood videos," Nurse Bailey said. "Abortion is not pretty. As we've talked about, it's not a decision that women take lightly."

"Well, it doesn't matter because I'm not doing it anyway," Shawna said. "I'm keeping my baby."

Ten

TWO MONTHS LATER, SHAWNA ENROLLED IN PRENATAL classes. Vivian took Shawna's hand as they approached the community center to attend their first class. Shawna looked at her mom, bemused.

"I'm your partner, sweetie," her mom said.

Shawna nodded. *Mom's hand feels so warm,* she thought. *Or maybe my hand is just cold.*

Shawna and her mom were greeted with warm smiles and she began to relax. Nurse Bailey was right about the prenatal class—there was an interesting mix of couples here. All skin colors and ages. *This might not be so bad after all.* All of the couples were holding hands and caressing each other. *Some of the women look even younger than me and some look old enough to be grandmothers,* Shawna thought. And then she realized her mom was about to become a grandmother. Shawna squeezed her mom's hand.

"Good evening, moms and partners," said Cindi, the instructor. Cindi wore yoga pants and had put her blonde hair in a high, tight ponytail off the top of her head. "Welcome to our first class. To start off, I want to go around the room and have everyone introduce themselves and tell us how you feel about having a baby."

Shawna felt that weird tightness in her chest again. She wasn't prepared for all the gushy, emotional crap. When it came to her turn she introduced herself. "And this is my mom, Vivian," she said, hoping to skip the feeling part.

"And what are your feelings about your baby?" Cindi asked.

"We're just so excited!" Vivian exclaimed. "It's a miracle!"

There was a murmur of agreement around the room.

Thanks, Mom, Shawna thought. *I'm glad somebody is excited.*

//

After class, her mom suggested they go for ice cream.

"Would you like Philippe to be your Lamaze partner?" her mom asked.

"Why would I?" Shawna asked.

"Do you think he'll want to be with you at the birth?" her mom asked. "I still feel a little uncomfortable with the way his parents behaved. But doesn't he want to be involved?"

"I think his parents are pissed about his 'involvement' to date," Shawna said. "If you catch my drift."

"I know, sweetie," her mom said. "They don't share my perspective. They haven't lost a child.

But I think we should at least invite Philippe to participate. If he says no, so be it."

//

When they got home Shawna texted Philippe.

Shawna: Hey.

Philippe: Yo.

Shawna: I went to my first prenatal class tonight. It's pretty cool. You learn all kinds of stuff about babies and shit. Do you want to go with me next week?

Philippe didn't respond. Shawna waited five minutes and texted again.

I guess that means no. I'm cool with that.

Philippe: I didn't say no.

Shawna: Is that a yes?

Philippe: I guess it's a maybe.

Shawna: I'm going in for an ultrasound tomorrow. Do you want to come? We'll actually see the kid. Find out if it's a girl or boy. Do you want to know?

Philippe: okay. I'll come. Tomorrow I mean.

Shawna crossed her legs and gritted her teeth. The doctor's office had told her not to pee until after the ultrasound. Her bladder needed to be full. *I am in agony!*

"I can't hold it much longer," Shawna said to Philippe. "I'm going to wet my pants right here in this waiting room!"

Philippe approached the receptionist. "How much longer? She really needs to pee."

The receptionist handed him a Dixie cup. "She can void about four ounces. No more."

Philippe walked back with the Dixie cup.

"Are you kidding me?" Shawna said. "Once I start to pee, there will be no stopping!"

Just then, the ultrasound technician called her name.

"Oh, thank God!" Shawna said. "I'm dying here."

"It will be a little better once you lie down," the

technician said. "Once we get the pictures, you can use the restroom. Trust me, it will be worth it."

Shawna hobbled after the technician and climbed onto the examining table. The nurse covered Shawna from the hips down with a paper sheet and pulled her top up to reveal her naval.

"This is going to be cold," the technician said. She squirted some gel on Shawna's belly.

"Holy shit!" Shawna exclaimed.

The technician peered into the monitor as she moved the paddle around Shawna's abdomen. Now and then, she stopped and pushed some buttons on the keyboard.

"He's doing somersaults," the technician exclaimed. "He won't stay still long enough for me to measure him."

"Him?" Shawna asked. "It's a boy?"

"I can't tell yet," the technician said. "I call them all he so I don't give anything away. Do you want to know the sex?"

"Yes," Shawna said.

"If we see a penis, I'll let you know," the technician said. "Sometimes it's hard to tell."

She pushed a little harder on the paddle and studied the screen. Suddenly, she hit a couple more keys. "There, got it."

"Everything look okay?" Shawna asked.

"Everything looks fine," the technician said. "Should I get the daddy?"

"Yes, thanks," Shawna said. *Daddy*, she thought. *Philippe is going to be a daddy! Now I understand why he is so freaked out.*

The technician swiveled the monitor so it was facing Shawna and then went to the door to call Philippe. He stood next to her and held her hand. Together they studied the dark clouds on the monitor.

"What are we looking at?" Philippe asked.

"Here's the head," the technician pointed to a dark area near the top of the screen. She moved the paddle around. "Here's an arm, here are the legs."

"I can't see anything," Shawna said.

"Me neither," Philippe said. "Oh wait. Is he sucking his thumb?"

"Yes, he is," the technician said.

Suddenly both Shawna and Philippe had a clear visual of their baby sucking his thumb. His head seemed much too big for his body.

"Whoa," Philippe said. "What's that, his penis?"

"You got it," the technician said. "It's a boy!"

"Oh my God!" Philippe was giggling and holding Shawna's hand in a death grip. Shawna had never seen him this way. Her heart swelled with emotion.

Shawna squinted at the screen. "Yes, I see it! It does look like he's sucking his thumb. Look! He's waving at us! Hi baby! Hi Sawyer!"

"Sawyer?" Philippe exclaimed. "What?"

"Some crazy name my mom dreamed up," Shawna said. "Sorry!"

"No way you're naming my baby Sawyer," Philippe said. "Jean-Jacques, maybe," he added, pronouncing it "janjak" in his French accent.

"Your baby?" Shawna said. She grinned from ear to ear. *I am having Philippe's baby!* "Oh man, I gotta pee so bad!"

"To your right," the technician said as Shawna bolted from the table.

Eleven

"**H**AVE YOU SPENT MUCH TIME AROUND BABIES, Shawna?" Nurse Bailey asked.

"Not really," she said. "I'm an only child. Apparently my mom wanted a second child but that didn't work out."

"What if I gave you a baby to take care of for a week?" Nurse Bailey asked.

"Huh?" Shawna said. "How does that work?"

"It's really kind of a game," Nurse Bailey said. She walked over to her cabinet.

"You have a baby in your cabinet?" Shawna asked.

Nurse Bailey smiled. "You'll see." She pulled a

bundle out of the cabinet. It was wrapped in a baby blanket. She handed it to Shawna. "Here you go. Here's your baby. He's a big one—ten pounds!"

Shawna took the bundle and looked at it. "What is this?" She pulled the blanket away and saw that she was holding a sack of flour.

"This is your newborn baby, Shawna," Nurse Bailey said.

"This is stupid," Shawna said. She shoved the bundle back at Nurse Bailey.

"I know it seems stupid, but humor me," Nurse Bailey said. "There's no real way of understanding the responsibility of being a mom until you've actually been one. All I want you to do is try it for one week. That's nothing considering that your real baby will be with you for twenty years at least."

Shawna sighed. "What do I have to do?"

Nurse Bailey rocked the sack of flour. "He's crying, Shawna."

Shawna rolled her eyes.

Nurse Bailey heaved the sack onto her shoulder

and began to pat it. "Maybe he's hungry. Or maybe his diaper is wet. What is your baby's name?"

"Jack," Shawna replied.

"You need to borrow some baby clothes for Jack and a couple of baby bottles and some toys. You'll also need to buy enough disposable diapers to last a week. That will be about fifty-six."

"Fifty-six diapers?" Shawna cried.

"Oh, yeah," Nurse Bailey said. "You need to change a newborn at least eight times a day. And you'll need to feed Jack every three hours and that will take roughly twenty minutes. So every three hours you need to stop whatever you're doing and feed Jack. Even at night. Set your alarm. You'll find out real soon why new moms suffer from depression. This is a hard job, Shawna—the hardest job on earth. And the most rewarding."

"I get it," Shawna said. "Keep your stupid flour sack."

"No. You don't get it," Nurse Bailey said. "It's one thing to know that a baby is a big responsibility.

It's another thing altogether to actually be responsible." She gingerly handed the bundle to Shawna. "Jack is crying. Try rocking him."

Shawna rolled her eyes but did as she was told. She stood up and rocked from side to side. She felt incredibly stupid.

"Jack must always be left with a responsible adult," Nurse Bailey said. "You can't ever leave him alone. If you go out, you must find a babysitter."

"I've got my mom," Shawna said.

"That's great," Nurse Bailey said. "But doesn't your mom work? Isn't she a professor?"

Shawna nodded.

"And sometimes Jack will cry for no apparent reason," Nurse Bailey said. "You've fed him, you've changed him, and still he's crying. What does he want? You might want to shake him to make him stop but that won't work and you could hurt him, badly. You need to hold him and rock him to soothe him."

Shawna began to rock the bundle a little harder, grateful, at least, that his nose wasn't running.

"Play with your baby," Nurse Bailey said. "Talk to your baby. You'd be surprised how many moms don't know that they must do that."

Shawna nodded.

"I'll give you a ride home after school," Nurse Bailey said. "And don't worry. I brought a car seat for Jack. You can borrow it for the week."

///

Shawna heard the doorbell ring. She threw off her comforter and trudged downstairs. It was Philippe.

"What do you want?" Shawna asked, not really interested.

"Can I come in?" Philippe asked.

Shawna shook her head. "I'm not supposed to have anyone in the house when my parents aren't home."

"Oh, c'mon," Philippe said. "What could

happen that hasn't already happened?" Philippe eyed Shawna's expanding belly.

"Shut up," Shawna said. "What do you want?'

"I came to help you find your sense of humor," Philippe said. "And to see how you and Jack are doing."

Shawna plunked herself down on the couch. She couldn't remember what day it was or the last time she had gone to class. She realized she'd been living in some kind of fog. She picked up the sack of flour, which she had dressed up in a onesie that she had found at the Goodwill store. She had drawn a smiley face on it with a Sharpie,

"What's that?" Philippe asked.

"It's Jack," Shawna said. "My practice baby."

"Can I hold him?" Philippe asked.

"Gladly." Shawna tossed the sack to him. "Cute, isn't he?"

"Very," Philippe said. He held the sack up to his shoulder and patted it. "Where did you get this?"

"Nurse Bailey," Shawna said. "How did you know how to hold him like that?"

"Please," Philippe said. "I have cousins and nephews. I've held a *lot* of babies."

"Nurse Bailey is trying to show me what it's like to be a mother," Shawna said. "She still thinks we should give Jack up for adoption."

"No way," Philippe said. "He's a good baby, right? Does he cry much?"

"He did at first," Shawna said. "But I straightened him out."

"What?" Philippe asked. "How did you do that?"

"I locked him in a closet."

Philippe doubled over in laughter.

Shawna handed him a bottle. "I'm supposed to feed him for twenty minutes every three hours and change his diaper eight times a day. But, frankly I think we should crack him open and make some pancakes."

"And there it is," Philippe said. "Your sense of humor. You're welcome."

"Are we making a mistake?" Shawna asked. "Let's face it. We're not ready to be parents. I mean I'm not sure if I'd ever be ready to sign up for this shit. I don't know how people do it. Babies suck!"

Twelve

"WHAT'S THE MATTER, SHAWNA?" HER MOM STOOD over the stove, stirring a big pot of soup.

"Why do you think something is wrong?" Shawna asked.

"You've been moping around all week. Something going on at school?"

"I feel like all of my friends are avoiding me," Shawna said. "Janna told me that her mom says she's not allowed to talk to me."

"That's terrible." Her mom held the spoon suspended over the pot and gave Shawna a worried look.

"I guess her parents think that she might start

having sex if she hangs out with me," Shawna said bitterly.

"More likely, seeing you scares them. They think, *There, but for the grace of God, goes our daughter.* People don't know what to say so they avoid the conversation. It's like when one of our friends says her husband is having an affair, everyone panics. Like it's a disease that they all could catch."

"Remember what you told me about getting pregnant at my age?" Shawna asked. "Did your friends shun you?"

"I only told one friend—Sheila. She was the one that drove me to San Francisco. We stayed friends until graduation. But we lost touch after I left for college. I think she's still in Fresno. You know what? I should look her up. She might even be on Facebook, right?"

"Probably. Everybody's mom is on Facebook," Shawna said. "You know what else bothers me? Everyone, even complete strangers, look at my stomach. Nobody looks me in the eye anymore. I can't figure out why I got pregnant in the first place, and not someone more deserving," Shawna said.

"More deserving? Like one of the couples who are desperate to adopt?"

"Yeah, or someone too stupid to use a condom," Shawna said. "We only did it once and we used a condom!"

//

Three months later, Dr. Hamersley frowned when she read the results of Shawna's blood pressure test at her weekly appointment.

"What's the matter?" Shawna asked.

"Your blood pressure is too high. It's a condition called pre-eclampsia." Dr. Hamersley squeezed Shawna's left ankle. The indentation took a little too long to return to normal. "Your swollen ankles are a symptom."

"What does that mean?"

"It's a complication that can lead to seizures and, rarely, coma. Usually we treat it with bed rest." Dr. Hamersley stared at Shawna's medical history on her computer. "I think we need to get you into the hospital."

"The hospital?" Shawna cried. "I'm going to the hospital already?"

"Anywhere between thirty-eight and forty-two weeks is considered full term," Dr. Hamersley explained. You're at thirty-eight weeks and your baby is large and healthy. We could induce tomorrow and he would be fine. It's your health that we're worried about. I'm admitting you to Alameda Hospital. You'll need to be there within an hour. Can someone drive you?"

"I'll text my mom," Shawna said.

//

Shawna sat in the lobby and waited until she saw her mom's car careen into the no-parking zone in front of the clinic. Her mom jumped out of the car, leaving the engine running as Shawna climbed into the passenger seat.

"I'm just going to run in and talk to Dr. Hamersley for a minute," her mom said. "I want to find out exactly what's going on."

"Mom!" Shawna said. "Please! We'll find out when we get to the hospital. Can we just go?" Shawna regretted her tone of voice but she was frustrated. Why did she have to calm her mom down instead of the other way around?

//

Shawna had been in the hospital for three days but things had only gotten worse. Her ankles were so swollen she no longer recognized her legs. *I look like an elephant!* Elephantitis—she'd heard the word and seen old ladies in the BART station. Her blood pressure was higher each time they measured it.

"So tomorrow is the day," Dr. Hamersley said. "Your baby's birthday will most likely be December second."

Shawna nodded. "A Sagittarius," she said. "Just like his dad." She was relieved to be getting it over with.

"Good. Tomorrow then, first thing, we'll start an IV and give you Pitocin. It's a natural hormone that induces labor. The contractions will start off mild but will increase in intensity. We'll give you an epidural for the pain, if necessary. It's not like what they taught you in your prenatal class. You'll need to stay in bed because we'll have a fetal monitor on the baby to make sure he's not in any distress."

"Can my mom and Philippe be here?" Shawna asked.

"Yes, unless there's an emergency that would require a Caesarian section," Dr. Hamersley said. "But I'm not anticipating that now."

Shawna nodded. Her whole body had started shaking involuntarily.

"Let's get you a little something to relax you," Dr. Hamersley said. "You'll need a good night's sleep."

Shawna had googled it. Induced labor could last anywhere from five to twenty-five hours. *This is it, Jack. We are in the show now—our very first rodeo. There is no going back.*

She tossed and turned, trying to sleep, but the drugs Dr. Hamersley gave her didn't seem to be working. She reached over to the phone on her nightstand and dialed the number.

"Hello?" Her mom answered after one ring, her voice anxious.

"Hi Mom," Shawna said. "It's me."

"Oh, I didn't recognize the number," her mom said. "Is everything okay?"

"Yeah. I just couldn't sleep. Did I wake you?" Shawna asked.

"No, Dad and I couldn't sleep either. We're sitting in the kitchen drinking herbal tea."

Shawna pictured them in the breakfast nook,

sitting across the table from each other. Suddenly she felt tears well up in her eyes. "I wish I was there with you," she said. "I feel so lonely here." She hated that her voice was quivering. *Why can't I control my emotions?!*

"Shawna," her mom said. "I'll be right there." Her mom's voice was shaking too.

"No, Mom," Shawna said. "I'm fine, really. I just wanted to call and tell you how much I love you and how sorry I am about all of this."

"Oh, sweetie," her mom said. "Do you want me to come stay with you tonight? I'm not going to be able to sleep anyway."

"No, it's okay." Shawna said.

"Everything is going to be fine."

"How do you know that?" Shawna asked. Her hands were shaking now and she realized that she was terrified about giving birth. "What if it's not?"

"Shawna," her mother said. "You have the best medical care in the bay area. Dr. Hamersley feels confident that everything will be fine. Dad and I will be there first thing in the morning."

"Okay." Shawna said. "See you tomorrow." She hung up the phone. *But I'm wide awake,* she thought. *How am I going to get through this night?*

Thirteen

SHAWNA WANDERED DOWN THE HALL TO THE NURSERY AND stood at the window, looking in. There weren't many babies in there and they were all sleeping soundly. A nurse moved from one bassinet to the next, checking on them. She spotted Shawna and pointed toward the door. Shawna walked toward the locked door and the nurse buzzed her in.

"I shouldn't let you in here," she said. "Put one of these on." She handed her a protective mask. "For germs. Are you having trouble sleeping?" the nurse asked.

Shawna nodded. It was warm in the nursery and the sweet smell of newborns filled the air.

"Are you having a C-section?" the nurse asked.

"No, I'm being induced tomorrow," Shawna replied. She stood beside a bassinet and looked down at a tiny, dark-skinned baby.

"So by tomorrow night, your baby will be here too," the nurse said. "Or maybe you'll want him to sleep in your room. A lot of moms do that even though keeping them here gives them a good night's sleep—it's often their last one for a while."

The baby in the bassinet started to squirm and punch the air with his tiny fists.

The nurse glanced at the clock. "It's time for his bottle. Do you want to watch me feed him?"

Shawna watched the baby as it woke up, his cries becoming raw and insistent. "Sure," she said. She wanted him to stop crying.

"Step back outside. You can watch through the window. I'm just going to wash my hands, and sit in that rocking chair right over there."

The nurse buzzed Shawna back out. She stood with her face pressed against the glass window, watching as the nurse grabbed the little bundle and held him close. She held the bottle and he latched on and began to suck right away, hungrily. *Jack, the sack of flour, wasn't anything like this. There really is no way to practice for this.* But then she realized that she would never even consider neglecting her real baby the way she neglected the sack of flour. *This little guy is a person—someone who is completely dependent on his mom. Where is his mom?*

She watched the nurse finish the bottle feeding and then expertly burp the baby. *How am I going to do that?* she wondered.

A moment later, the nurse was outside of the nursery sitting on a bench next to Shawna.

"Where is that little guy's mother?" Shawna asked. "Shouldn't she be breastfeeding?"

"I shouldn't be telling you this," she paused. "This little guy is being adopted," the nurse said. "His mom didn't even want to see him. She felt it would be too hard to let him go. It will be just bottles for him."

She kept staring at the baby through the pane of glass. She sensed he knew that the nurse wasn't his mom, but he didn't mind her feeding him. *I guess this would be the story of the rest of his life.* She leaned over and pressed her face close to the glass, for the first time in her life, wanting very badly to hold a baby.

"You have an awesome job," Shawna said. "All these babies."

There was a long and awkward pause. Finally Shawna broke it, "I'm just so scared," she said.

The nurse just smiled. "Of course you are. Like every expectant mother in the world. You'll be fine," she said.

"I practiced with a sack of flour," Shawna said.

"Tomorrow, you'll be holding the real thing," the nurse said.

"Yes," Shawna said, and a full-mouth smile crept up on her.

//

A nurse woke Shawna up in the middle of the night. At least it seemed like the middle of the night. Her nametag said Rose Ryan, RN, and her face was puffy and arms were beefy, like a Mrs. Potato Head doll.

"Time to induce," Nurse Ryan said.

She swabbed Shawna's arm with something cold.

Shawna recoiled at the sight of the IV kit and its needle.

"This will only sting for a second," Nurse Ryan said.

Shawna shut her eyes—she couldn't stand the sight of needles. She felt the prick of the needle and then heard a soft click and then the crinkling of the kit's wrappers. Nurse Ryan was humming a tune, as if performing some everyday task, like washing dishes.

"Aren't you going to take the needle out?" Shawna asked.

Nurse Ryan seemed to think that was funny.

"The needle *is* out, hon. What's left inside your vein is a catheter. It's attached to the tubing that connects to the IV, which has the Pitocin. That's the stuff that's gonna help put you into labor. We're also giving you magnesium sulfate to prevent seizures. Didn't your doctor discuss this with you?"

"Yes," Shawna said. "I thought it would be a shot or a pill or something."

"We'll need to monitor your contractions and dial the Pitocin up or down as needed," Nurse Ryan said. "Let me know when you start to feel something."

Nothing happened for awhile, and Shawna woke up feeling hot, and slightly sick. There was also a clenching pain. It rolled across her like someone had kicked her hard. But then it kept on. The pain didn't come and go, it grabbed her and held on. Shawna moaned and tried to roll over her side.

"Honey, we gotta keep the monitor on you," Nurse Ryan said, re-adjusting the fetal monitor attached to her belly, and watching the computer monitor to make sure the heartbeat started recording again. "There we go. Is your birth partner here?"

"My mom is coming," Shawna said. "I hope. I didn't know we were going to start this without her. I don't feel so good. I'm all sweaty."

"That's the magnesium sulfate. I can get you some ice chips."

Ice chips? Shawna thought, feeling another contraction. "Owwwww, here comes another one."

Shawna felt her stomach become hard and tight. The pain started big and then got bigger and bigger. Shawna felt like she was being ripped in two with a jagged saw that was inside of her. She knew she wasn't going to survive and she wanted it over fast. She reached out to grasp Nurse Ryan's arm. "Can they give something?" she gasped. "Something to knock me out? Something for the pain?"

The next contraction caught Shawna by surprise. She gritted her teeth and tried not to scream.

She wasn't even relieved when the pain stopped because she knew there would be another, and another.

She tried to pretend she was somewhere else, at the beach with Philippe, but it didn't work. She thought she heard someone screaming and then she realized it was her.

"Can't I have something for the fucking pain?" Shawna cried.

"I paged the anesthesiologist," Nurse Ryan said. "He'll be here shortly."

Shortly? Shawna wondered. *My body is being ripped apart!*

Another contraction hit and Nurse Ryan disappeared. Shawna was lost in a world of pain and bright lights. She could hear the screams again but mostly she was floating away. Every time she opened her eyes, the room whirled around so she kept them shut tight. In her mind she kept trying to run away but the pain kept catching up, slamming into her and refusing to let her go.

Weeks later, when Shawna would look back on the morning of December second, only a blur of images would come to mind. Like the faces of the people who came and went: her mom and dad, Philippe and his mom, Dr. Hamersley, and the ever-changing parade of nurses checking on her, monitoring her progress. She saw herself as if from a distance—an out-of-body experience—lying on the bed, hot, sweaty, nauseous, shocked with the intensity of the contractions.

At the height of the pain, her memory became even hazier. She vaguely remembered being told it was time to push. Finally, when she thought she had no more strength, the last horrific push came and she felt the baby slipping out of her, sudden and anti-climatic. Once his shoulders were out, Jack slipped out so easily. And then Dr. Hamersley was stitching her up. She could no longer feel a thing down there.

That was where the jumble of memories ended.

Fourteen

THE NEXT TIME SHE OPENED HER EYES, THE ROOM WAS in shadows. Her eyes ached as she squinted to see in the dimness. Philippe was slumped over in a chair across the room and she rubbed her eyes to see him more clearly. The lamp next to the bed made a small circle of light.

She woke up a little at a time. Her body hurt all over and her head was pounding. She knew where she was but she couldn't remember what had happened.

"Did I have the baby?" Her voice came out in a croak. She touched her stomach. It felt loose and flabby. It reminded her of a balloon that someone had let the air out of. *Of course I had the baby,* she thought. *My body is empty.* "Did I kill it?"

Philippe approached the bed. "You're awake!" he said.

"Where's my baby?" Shawna asked. "Is he okay?"

"He's fine," Philippe said, stroking her arm. "He's in the nursery getting cleaned up. I'll let the nurse know you're awake. That was pretty rough there toward the end. The doctor was threatening to perform a C-section. All that blood! It was like a slasher movie. And then you fell asleep."

"What time is it?" Shawna asked.

"It's about seven," Philippe said. "Jack was born thirty minutes ago. You held him for a minute, but you were so tired that they thought you should rest. Anyway, you passed out like a minute later."

"I want to see him again," Shawna said.

"I'll go get him," Philippe said and left the room. He returned with a nurse rolling a bassinet. She positioned the bassinet next to Shawna's head.

"Here, let's sit you up so you can hold him,"

the nurse said. "Do you want to try to breast feed now?"

The nurse raised the head of Shawna's bed and positioned her pillows to prop her up. She gingerly picked up the sleeping baby and showed Shawna how to support his head.

The surge of love Shawna felt for the tiny, wrinkled baby in her arms was staggering. She realized at that moment that she had never felt love before. *Not love like this.* There was nothing that could ever come close to the love she was feeling. She stared into the baby's face, dumbstruck by the overwhelming power of the moment. This was the baby that she and Philippe had created and her body had nurtured from a mass of cells to this, a perfectly-formed human being. This was the baby that she had visualized and talked to, that had occupied one hundred percent of her bandwidth for so many months. Shawna pulled back Jack's tiny knitted cap. A mass of wet black hair stuck to his head. Shawna loosened the blanket and Jack drew out an arm. His tiny clenched fist immediately found its way to his mouth and his thumb popped right in.

Shawna looked up at Philippe. "Just like in the ultrasound image," she said.

Philippe was struggling to maintain his composure. He had been strong for her all day but now he looked exhausted and emotional, like he was going to collapse.

Shawna carefully scooted over on the bed. "Sit down," she said. Philippe climbed in.

"Do you want to hold him?" Shawna asked.

Philippe nodded and took the baby from her. "He's perfect," Philippe said.

"Yes," Shawna said. "Just like you."

//

Shawna spent the rest of the night nudging Jack onto her nipple. He eventually latched on, squeaking a little as he sucked. At some point Shawna fell asleep with Jack splayed across her chest. She awoke to the sound of her mother entering her room.

Vivian had brought daisies and a bag filled with sparkling water, pretzels, and Milano cookies. "I tried to guess what you would be craving," she said looking at Philippe who was asleep in the chair. "I'll only stay a few minutes but I wanted to see my grandson."

Philippe woke up. "I couldn't believe what she went through," he said. "I thought her eyes were going to pop out."

"When the baby came out, did he look angry or worried?" her mom asked.

"I don't know," Shawna said. "When I saw him after I woke up—the part that I remember more clearly—I guess he just looked curious."

Her mom picked up the baby and rocked him.

"Mom, he should eat again," Shawna said. Her mom carried the baby over and placed him on Shawna's chest.

Shawna pushed Jack's face onto her nipple, which was already sore. "Ow, when do you get used to this?" she asked.

"Your nipples will toughen up," her mom said.

Just then, the door swung open and Philippe's parents walked in with a basket from the local deli. Shawna hadn't seen them since the "garden party" as she had taken to calling it.

"I figured you could use more food than flowers," Mrs. Henri said.

Vivian stood up. "David, Gaby," she said tightly.

They all stood there until Philippe went over to hug his parents. Shawna desperately wanted to cover up but Jack was sucking hungrily on her nipple. The room felt too warm and too crowded.

Mrs. Henri walked over to look at the baby's face. Mr. Henri, thankfully hung back.

"He's beautiful," Gaby said, matter-of-factly, switching a smile on and off. "What's his name?"

Shawna and her mom spoke in unison. "Sawyer!" Vivian said.

"Jack!" Shawna said.

"What?" her mom asked. "I thought we agreed on Sawyer?"

"Mom, we never agreed on anything," Shawna said. "Philippe and I chose Jack."

"Jack," Gaby sniffed. "That sounds Irish. Can I hold him?"

"I think he is finished," Shawna said. She yanked at her gown to cover her chest. "Can you burp him? There's a cloth on the end of the bed."

Mrs. Henri draped the cloth over her shoulder and held Jack to her chest, gently bouncing and patting him until he gave a little burp. She cradled the baby in her arms and gazed lovingly down at him. Mr. Henri beamed over her shoulder. They looked like your average, over-the-moon grandparents. Not angry at all, at least not in the moment.

"He's got Philippe's eyes," Gaby murmured.

"Can I get you anything, Shawna?" her mom said as she headed for the door.

"You're leaving?" Shawna asked. *Leaving me alone with Philippe's family!* she thought.

"Dad will be back tomorrow morning to pick you up," her mom said. "Call me if you need anything."

"We should be leaving, too," Gaby said. "Are you coming, Philippe?"

"I'm staying, Mom," Philippe said. "I'll be home tomorrow."

Fifteen

"WHEN CAN YOU LEAVE?" PHILIPPE STOOD OVER Shawna, stroking Jack's head.

"Not sure," Shawna said. "I think the doctor has to give the okay and then we sign out. My dad is supposed to be here by ten."

"I'll go ask," Philippe said.

It seemed like he was gone forever and when Philippe finally returned he was sweating. Shawna worried if it was too hot outside for Jack.

"There was a shitload of paperwork," Philippe said. He stared at Jack again. "He's so tiny. Do you think it's safe to take him home?"

"Can you hold him?" Shawna said. "I need to pack up."

Shawna passed Jack to Philippe and he held the baby gingerly in the crook of his arm. Shawna collected her toiletries and tossed them into her backpack.

"You think he's eating enough?" Philippe asked anxiously. "He sleeps all the time."

"The nurse said to feed him every three hours," Shawna. "The book said he is supposed to sleep eighteen hours a day."

"Don't you think he would want to be awake and see what's going on after being stuck in there for so long?" Philippe asked, eyeing her sagging belly. "Can you imagine how boring it must have been? Nine months—sheesh!"

"Tell me about it," Shawna said.

"Rise and shine, buddy." Philippe held Jack upright. "Look at the world."

"Ready to go?" The nurse stood in the doorway with a wheelchair.

"A wheelchair? Seriously?" Shawna said. "I can walk."

"Hospital rules," the nurse said.

Shawna climbed into the wheelchair and Philippe placed Jack in her arms. Shawna looked up at Jack and felt a force field surround the three of them. *My own little family,* she thought.

Outside, Shawna's dad was waiting by the car, pointing a video camera in their direction.

"Perfect," he said. "I got all three of you." He continued to film as Philippe buckled Jack in the car seat. It was like her dad couldn't take the camera away from his face and just look at the baby.

"Hey there, little man," he said to the baby. He finally shut off the camera and looked at Shawna. "How are you feeling?"

"Fine," she said. "Glad to be going home." Actually, she felt all banged up and contorted inside.

Shawna got into the passenger seat and Philippe leaned in for a kiss. "I guess I'll see you when I see you," she said. It felt weird going home alone with her baby. Philippe would go back to his house and they would both be starting classes in a few weeks—at different colleges. Shawna was going to Berkeley on her mother's employee scholarship and Philippe was starting his second semester at San Francisco State, across the bay.

Shawna's dad put his foot on the clutch and the car lurched out of the parking lot. "I read that you're supposed to walk the baby around the house and introduce him to everything," he said.

"What?" Shawna said. "Where did you read that?"

"You never know how much they are taking in," he said. His voice was weirdly animated, like he was a game show host trying to psyche up his contestants. Shawna felt a pang of appreciation that he was being such a good sport. He had been opposed to the pregnancy the whole time. "I always thought you were wise beyond your years when you were a baby."

"I wish I could remember that," Shawna said.

"You and mom bringing me home from the hospital."

"I remember it like it was yesterday," he said. "Your mom was on cloud nine."

"No post-partum blues?" Shawna asked.

"She really wanted to have more kids but she had a hard time getting pregnant again," he said. "There were several tough years—miscarriages."

"I know," Shawna said. "She told me."

"Did she?" he mused.

When they got to the house, her dad made a big deal of holding open doors and looking for ways to be useful. He unbuckled Jack's car seat and carried it inside, looking for a place to set it down. He finally nestled it into a crook of the couch and set Shawna's bag down next to it.

Shawna's mom rushed in from the kitchen. "You're here! Let me see my grandson."

"Thanks Mom, I'm fine," Shawna said sarcastically. She stomped upstairs to her room and collapsed on her bed. She drifted off to sleep and dreamt that she was back in high school. Before. Before all of this had happened. All of her friends from high school were like ghosts in her head, conversing and floating around. Talking about boys and dating and applying to college—moving away from home and doing all the normal teenage things.

In her dream she was a freshman again, filled with excitement and awe at traversing the halls in the big high school building. It was early October and the air was bright and crisp, and a brisk breeze was blowing in from the bay. She was in biology class when the fire alarm went off and she filed outside on to the front lawn with the rest of her class. *Why don't they have fire drills during first period when everyone still has their coats?* she wondered. She huddled behind a tree to block the wind and as she studied the gloomy, red-bricked façade of the school for any signs of a real fire, she spotted him. Philippe was leaning against the wall, hugging himself in a thin, black sweater. He was tall and had large, square shoulders, unlike the other skinny freshman boys who had yet to experience their first growth spurt. *This guy looks too old for high school,* she thought. Shawna looked around for someone she knew, someone to talk to, but she was surrounded by kids from her biology class, most of whom were sophomores.

One minute Philippe was watching her from afar and the next he appeared beside her, as if in a blink.

"I did it," he said.

"Did what?" Shawna laughed.

"I pulled the alarm," Philippe said. "I knew I would find you here. So I pulled the alarm."

"You did not!" Shawna hopped from foot to foot.

"Are you cold?" Philippe asked. "Do you want my sweater?"

"Do you have anything on underneath?" Shawna asked.

Just then the bell rang, indicating the all clear, and the students filed back into the building.

"What's your name?" he asked as they parted ways in the corridor.

Off in the distance, Shawna heard a baby crying. *Why is there a baby in the high school?* The noise seemed to be coming closer and then she heard her mom's voice.

"Shawna, wake up. The baby is hungry. Shawna . . . "

Sixteen

SIX MONTHS LATER, SHAWNA WAS ALMOST HOME WHEN she remembered they were out of diapers. *Shit!* She had promised her mom that she would pick them up after class. So she doubled back to the Safeway on Alameda. Jack had fallen asleep in his car seat and as she parked the car, she thought that it would have been a whole lot easier to just leave him in the car while she ran into the store, but she knew she couldn't do that.

Jack woke up as soon as she unbuckled him. Shawna held her breath, afraid that he might start to cry. But he just grinned and made a happy squeal as Shawna buckled him facing outward into the Baby Bjorn. Jack loved being carried around facing out so he could look at people's faces.

Shawna hated walking around in public with Jack. She hated the way people stared at her, always stopping to comment and ask whose baby he was. She was aware that his skin was so much darker than hers. *People are so rude,* she thought.

She headed straight to the baby aisle and grabbed a jumbo pack of diapers and threw in some wipes and baby shampoo and baby powder and formula. *Shit, I should have made a list.* She tallied the amount in her head, worried she might not have enough money on her debit card. The Henris had agreed to split the baby expenses and had set up a dedicated bank account but Philippe didn't always remember to make the deposits.

Shawna was headed for the checkout when she saw Caroline Luft's mother coming out of the produce section. Caroline and Shawna had played soccer together all through middle school. Shawna knew the look she would get and that tone of pity in her voice.

Shawna whipped into the next aisle and Jack let out a whoop and a big, juicy fart. "Not now, Jack!" Shawna hissed. She found herself in the cereal aisle. She slowed down, pretending to peruse the selection of Kashi and Granola, hoping Mrs. Luft would be checked out and on her way to her car.

Jack started to squirm—he needed a diaper change. Shawna made a dash for the express lane.

The checkout lady smiled at Jack. "Aren't you a cutie?" she said. She looked up a Shawna. Here we go, thought Shawna. "Is this your little brother?" the clerk asked.

Shawna nodded and averted her eyes. There was just enough money on the debit card to cover her purchases. She would have to call Philippe to remind him to make another deposit. She hated asking him for money. He would have to go ask his father and then there would always be an argument. Shawna suspected that the Henris set it up this way to extract the most pain from her and Philippe—a daily reminder of their irresponsibility.

When she got home, Shawna thought about putting Jack in his high chair with a bottle and some crackers—or maybe even sticking him in his crib. Just so she could get some things done, like her homework, or washing her hair. But Nurse Bailey had told her that playing with Jack was one of the things she was supposed to do.

The living room was crammed with baby stuff that her mother had bought at yard sales—a swing, a jumper chair, a cradle, and a blanket spread out on the floor that was littered with rattles and stuffed animals.

Shawna changed Jack, put him down on the blanket and turned on the radio. The parenting book had said music was good for a baby's mental development. They played chase the baby around the living room. Jack had just learned how to crawl and loved being chased by Shawna on her hands and knees. They played the game until Jack collapsed on the floor, rolled onto his back, and fell asleep.

Shawna sat there and watched him to make sure he wasn't going to wake up. She eyed her backpack by the front door and thought about pulling out her Economics assignment; she thought about sneaking upstairs to take a shower. In the end, she curled up next to Jack and fell asleep, too.

Her mom walked in the door and woke Shawna up.

"What time is it?" Shawna asked, rubbing her eyes.

"Six-thirty," her mom said.

Shawna looked over at Jack who was still asleep. "Jesus, we have been asleep for over an hour. I should wake him up or he will keep me up all night."

"I brought home Mexican," her mom said. "Let's eat before he wakes up."

Shawna scrambled to her feet. "Mexican! I'm starving."

They sat at the kitchen table and Shawna wolfed down a burrito.

"Did you eat today?" her mom asked.

"Um." Shawna couldn't remember. Jack had woken up twice in the night to nurse. She had slept through her alarm and didn't have time to shower before dropping Jack at the on-campus daycare center and dashing to her first class at Berkeley.

"You need to eat," her mom said. "You've lost so much weight. How much longer do you plan to breastfeed?"

"The book says a year would be ideal," Shawna said. "But already I feel like I can't keep up with him. He's always hungry. I bought some formula today. The kind the doctor recommended."

"I'll fix him a bottle," her mom said. "Why don't you jump in the shower?"

"Thanks, Mom!" Shawna said, exhausted. "I'll

get the dishes and start a load of laundry before Dad gets home."

"Don't you have homework?" her mom asked.

"Yeah, that too," Shawna said.

///

When Shawna got out of the shower, her mom was sitting on the sofa with Jack, reading him a *Pat the Bunny* pop-up book. She had bathed him and changed him. He was contentedly patting the furry pages and nuzzling his head against Vivian's chest. He didn't even look up when Shawna entered the room and she felt a pang of jealousy.

"Mom, I can do that," Shawna said.

"No, you need to do your homework," her mom said. "How are your grades this semester?"

"Dad's not home yet?" Shawna asked to change the subject.

"He's in Sacramento, working on a case," her mom said. "I'm not sure if he'll be home tonight."

"He's out of town a lot these days," Shawna said.

Her mom shot her a sharp look so Shawna quietly retrieved her backpack and retreated to her bedroom to study. She fell asleep with her Shakespeare book splayed on her chest and all the lights on.

//

When Shawna dropped Jack off at daycare the next morning, Mrs. Brawley, the director, stopped her at the door.

"Shawna, did you bring extra diapers today?" she asked. "You forgot them yesterday."

"I know," Shawna said. "We were out. I bought some on the way home yesterday. See?" Shawna brandished a bundle labeled with Jack's name. Several other moms walked in while they were standing there. The other moms all greeted each other and their babies. All of the other moms and dads were either graduate students or employees in their late twenties and thirties. Nobody ever greeted Shawna unless it was Mrs. Brawley scolding her for some new infraction. She felt like she was invisible. Only the girls who worked there were close to her age and at least once a week some parent would approach her with their snotty-faced kid and ask, "Do you work here?" *No! I don't fucking work here,* she wanted to scream.

Seventeen

WHEN SHE WALKED INTO HER LITERATURE CLASS, everyone was already engaged in a lively conversation about Iago being just another side of Othello's character. Shawna ducked her head and hoped the instructor wouldn't call on her. She kicked herself for falling asleep the night before and not finishing reading the play. She vowed to do better—to get Jack on a sleep schedule so she could put him down at a reasonable hour and she would have time to study and still get enough sleep.

At noon, she ran back to the daycare center to nurse Jack. Judy, one of the workers, had him sitting in a high chair munching on Cheerios.

"Isn't he cute?" Judy asked.

Actually I think he is fucking brilliant. It seemed like just yesterday he had been lying around on his back, hitting himself in the head with his own fist. Now, here he was picking up a Cheerio and sucking on it. She felt like she was missing out on everything. One minute he was smearing juice and crackers in his hair, and the next he was feeding himself Cheerios.

Shawna's breasts were full and aching. "I need to nurse," she said to Judy.

"I'm not sure he will be hungry," Judy said. "But you can try."

Thanks! Shawna fumed. *Why are you feeding my baby fucking Cheerios when you know I'll be here at noon to nurse him? Why does it seem like everyone, including my mother, is undermining me, making me feel inadequate, let's face it—irrelevant?*

//

That night, Shawna was trying to simultaneously breastfeed Jack and read Shakespeare when the phone rang.

"Hey. It's me," Philippe said.

"Hey." Shawna cradled the phone between her shoulder and ear and closed Shakespeare. "What's up?"

"I had this great idea," Philippe said.

Shawna smiled. One thing she really appreciated about Philippe was his enthusiasm. "What's that?" she asked. She leaned over and wiped Jack's face with a wet washcloth.

"I was thinking we could go to the Dreadmau5 concert on Treasure Island this weekend," Philippe said.

Jack had grabbed the washcloth and was sucking on it. Shawna immediately thought of all the reasons that she couldn't—she'd promised to vacuum and clean the bathroom. There was laundry, homework, Jack. Worst of all, she had no money. This seemed like a terrible time, but she had to bring it up.

"Um, Philippe," she said. "That sounds like so much fun but I'd need to find a sitter and um . . ."

"You need money," Philippe said flatly.

"Yeah, sorry," Shawna said.

"What if my mom takes Jack this weekend?" he asked.

Shawna panicked. Leave Jack with Mrs. Henri? "Really? She said she'd do that?"

"My mom's been asking me to ask you for a while," Philippe said. "I think she wants to share custody."

The words were stuck in her throat. "What do you mean, share?" Shawna was finally able to choke out.

"You know," Philippe said. "Like joint custody."

"Do you have any idea what you are asking?" Shawna exclaimed. "You would be the one that I would be sharing custody with. Do you even know how hard it is to take care of a baby? I haven't had more than four hours of sleep since Jack was born."

"I thought your mom was taking care of him," Philippe said.

"Sure, she helps feed him and bathe him, sometimes," Shawna said, now angry. *Why does everyone assume I am incapable of being a mother?* "I drop him at daycare on campus every morning. I nurse him three times in between classes and then I pick him up by five every night. He wakes up at least twice in the middle of the night to nurse some more. Are you up for that? Is your mom really going to get up at one a.m. to give him a bottle? Are you?"

"How are you getting your homework done?" Philippe asked.

There was silence on the line.

"Are you still there?" Philippe asked.

"I'm not," Shawna said. "Getting my homework done, I mean. I keep falling asleep in the middle of doing my homework. I think I'm going to need to drop a couple of classes this semester. I am so far behind on the reading."

"Wow," Philippe said. "I had no idea."

"Tell your mom, if she wants to babysit on Saturday while we're at the concert, fine," Shawna said, wearily. "After babysitting for one day, she may change her mind about custody. Especially if you make it clear that she would be doing all the work so that you can stay focused on your school work."

///

On Saturday, Philippe picked up Shawna and Jack. Shawna handed him the car seat and the stroller. She had Jack strapped into his Baby Bjorn and had an enormous diaper bag slung over her shoulder.

"What is all this shit?" Philippe exclaimed.

"Babies have lots of baggage," Shawna said. "We should also grab the playpen and bouncy seat. Your mom will need a place to put him if she needs to pee or answer the phone or whatever. Of course, if your mom wants to make this a regular thing, she can buy her own crib and stuff so we won't have to lug everything over there every time."

While Shawna strapped the car seat into the back seat, Philippe loaded everything else into the trunk of his car. When they arrived at his house, he reversed the process, making three trips to the front porch to deposit everything.

"Hey, Mom!" he yelled through the screen door. "We're here. Where do you want all this stuff?"

His mother came to the door. "Oh my goodness! What is all this?"

"Baby baggage," Philippe said. "Where do you want it?"

"Put everything in the living room," Mrs. Henri said. "Did you bring diapers and a change of clothes?"

"Everything is in here," Shawna handed Mrs. Henri the diaper bag. "Hi, Mr. Henri!"

Mr. Henri didn't respond. He stood up from his chair and stalked into the kitchen, deliberately ignoring all of them.

"There are three bottles of formula in there—you need to refrigerate those. You can warm them in the microwave. He will start fussing around five and then again at eight and eleven. We should be back before the two a.m. feeding, right, Philippe?"

Shawna went out to the car to get Jack out of the car seat. "Philippe, can you grab the car seat? Your mom might want to go out."

Shawna carried Jack into the house on her hip.

"There's my beautiful grandson!" Mrs. Henri exclaimed. She took the baby from Shawna and Jack started to wail.

"Let's distract him," Shawna said. She spread out a blanket on the floor and put his favorite stuffed bunny on it alongside a rattle and a ball with bells inside that rang when you rolled it. Mrs. Henri put Jack down on the blanket. He grabbed the bunny and started chewing on an ear.

Shawna pulled the *Pat the Bunny* book from the diaper bag. "He loves it when my mom reads this to him. He also likes *Wheels on the Bus*. I put everything you will need in the diaper bag. But you can call me if you have any questions. You have my number, right?"

Eighteen

"**H**AVE FUN!" MRS. HENRI CALLED AND WAVED AS THEY left the house.

As they were pulling out of the driveway, Shawna said, "What's up with your dad?"

"Man, he is so pissed about all of this," Philippe said.

"All of what?" Shawna asked.

"You, me, Jack," Philippe said. "He doesn't want to pay child support. They fight about it a lot. I wish I was done with school and working so they wouldn't have to be involved at all. What did your mom say about leaving the baby with my mom?"

"I didn't tell her," Shawna said.

"What?" Philippe said. "Where does she think he is?"

"I don't know," Shawna said. "I don't care. Jack is my baby, not hers."

"What is going on?" Philippe asked.

"Last night my mom and I were screaming at each other about rice cereal. Can you believe that?" Shawna said. "She bosses me around all day and night, telling me what is best for my son. I am killing myself trying to stay in college and care for him and once in a while she reads him a book or gives him a bath, all the while trying to show me that she is so much better at parenting than I am."

They rode in silence for a few miles.

"The concert should be fun," Philippe ventured.

"You remember when she said she wanted to raise the baby?" Shawna said. "Well there is a reason behind that. And you can never share this with anyone. Not *anyone*, you promise?"

"I promise," Philippe said.

"Not even my dad knows about this," Shawna said.

"Whoa. What is it?" Philippe asked.

"My mom got pregnant at seventeen and she had an abortion," Shawna said. "She lied to her boyfriend and told him that she had miscarried. Isn't that evil?"

"Her boyfriend never even had a say in it?" Philippe asked.

"He even offered to marry her," Shawna said. "So now she believes that Jack is God's little messenger to her, saying that He has forgiven her. She wants to believe that she is raising my baby to make herself feel better, I guess."

"That's fucking twisted," Philippe said.

"She is nuts," Shawna said. "She would have a conniption if she knew your mom was babysitting. Ha! I'll show her."

//

Treasure Island was a mob scene. Shawna got caught up in the energy of it all. It had been so long since she had just been a kid, dancing with abandon—without a care in world. She wished it could always be like this with nothing else to think about except the music and the crowd and her heart beating inside her chest.

///

They got back to Philippe's house at eleven thirty and Mrs. Henri was pacing the living room floor with Jack in her arms. He was squalling.

"Mom," Philippe said, "Is everything okay?"

"Where have you been?" Mrs. Henry hissed. "He's been crying for hours. I haven't been able to console him and your father is beside himself."

"Why didn't you call us?" Shawna asked. She took Jack from Mrs. Henri's arms and his howling quieted to a whimper.

"I knew you hadn't been out in months," Mrs. Henri said. "You deserved a little time off."

Shawna was shocked. She had always thought that Philippe's mom hated her. Even her own mother would never acknowledge that Shawna needed some alone time.

"I wish I was a better grandmother," Mrs. Henri said. "I fed him, I changed him, I rocked him. Nothing seemed to work."

"I'm sure you're a wonderful grandma," Shawna said. She cradled Jack in her arms and gave Mrs. Henri a sympathetic look. "This was his first time away from home or daycare. We should have started with a shorter play date to help him get acclimated."

"I guess the custody idea is out the window?" Philippe asked.

His mom gave Philippe a sharp look.

"It's okay. Philippe told me that you would like to share custody," Shawna said. "I am open to the idea, when Jack is a little older. But, maybe we could plan weekly visits for now? You could take him for a couple of hours on Sunday afternoon so I could catch up on my homework?"

"I would love that," Mrs. Henri said. "But what will your mother say?"

"She will have a stroke," Shawna said. She shared a conspiratorial grin with Philippe. "But it's not really her decision."

//

By Tuesday, Shawna was well in to her routine of sleep deprivation and irritability. She picked up Jack from daycare and schlepped him home for another round of eating and shitting and laundry and dirty dishes.

"I have to say, baby," Shawna said. "I am kind of pissed at the way you rule my life; I can't do anything I want to do for more than three seconds without you flipping out. I am stuck with you all the time while everyone else, including your fucking father, has a life." Shawna imagined Philippe shuffling across campus in his flip-flops, snacking on his Red Bull and Clif Bars. She was sure he wasn't thinking about her and Jack twenty-four-seven.

She put Jack in his bouncy seat on the bathroom floor and ran the tub to bathe him. She was lowering him into the tub when her cell phone went off in her pocket. As she reached for it, Jack slipped out of her grasp and into the scalding water. She had forgotten to test the temperature. Jack started screaming bloody murder and she snatched him out of the tub. His legs were bright red. Shawna dipped her elbow in the water and screamed, "Too hot, too hot, too hot!"

Shawna grabbed her phone. "Hello, hello," she screamed.

"It's mom," Vivian said. "Did you . . . ?"

"Mom!" Shawna cried. "I burned Jack's legs with hot water. What do I do?"

"Fill the tub with cold water, and put him in,"

she said. "Cool but not too cold. Keep him there for a few minutes if you can. How bad is it?"

"I don't know," Shawna yelled.

Vivian sounded a little panicked. "Well, call a cab and get him to the hospital. I'll meet you there."

Shawn drained the hot water and held Jack under the tub faucet by the armpits, almost grateful that he was screaming and crying because it meant he wasn't dying. At the same time she noticed something weird. She wasn't panicking. She felt insanely calm and knew exactly what to do. He would be okay. She wrapped Jack in a diaper and a blanket and ran downstairs to meet the cab.

"Where to?" the cab driver asked.

"Emergency room," Shawna said, still calm. Then, "Oh shit, I don't have any money!"

"No problem," the cab driver said and switched off his meter. He handed her his business card, "You can pay me back."

A man in blue scrubs met them as they pulled

into the carport and pried Jack from Shawna's arms. He ran inside and disappeared behind some locked doors. She paced in the lobby, pinching the flesh on her arms, saying to herself, *please God, please God, please God.* The door swung open and in ran her mother.

Shawna followed her mom along the orange line painted on the tile floor and around a corner where they nearly bumped into a woman in green scrubs. Jack was lying on a cot with metal rails, wailing and writhing.

"I'm Dr. Tracy," the woman said. "Did you give him anything? Tylenol?"

"I tried to get him to swallow some liquid Tylenol," Shawna said. "Can you give him something for the pain? Something to make him stop screaming?"

Oh, my poor little Jack! What have I done? Please God, let him be okay. I should call Philippe.

Nineteen

THE DOCTOR WAS HOLDING JACK'S LEG AND STRAIGHTENING it. She inspected his skin, which was still bright red, and dotted with large blisters. "Second-degree burns," she said.

"What does that mean?" Shawna asked.

"First degree is like a bad sunburn," Dr. Tracy said. "Second degree involves some blistering but will heal by itself without requiring skin grafts. He won't have permanent scars. It's gonna be okay."

"Oh, thank God," Shawn said.

As Dr. Tracy dabbed at the wounds, Jack started screaming again and tried to pull his foot out of her hand.

"Isn't there something you can give him?" Shawna asked again.

Dr. Tracy pulled a tube out of a drawer. "This will numb the area and prevent infection." Jack screamed while she applied the gel but then quieted down once she was done. Dr. Tracy finished wrapping Jack's burns with gauze and looked at Shawna.

"What exactly happened?" she asked.

"The bathtub water was too hot," Shawna said. "He was only in it for a second, I swear!"

Dr. Tracy put her hand up. "On second thought, I think I need to find someone who can speak with you in private."

"I forgot to test it with my elbow before I put him in," Shawna said. "I always test the water."

"Wait, please," Dr. Tracy said. From the look on her face, Shawna knew that Dr. Tracy thought she had burned Jack on purpose.

Vivian spoke up. "We'll speak to whomever you need us to."

"Are you nursing him?" Dr. Tracy asked.

"Yes," Shawna said.

"You might want to nurse him right now," Dr. Tracy said. "To calm him. He's probably more scared than hurt right now."

Shawna picked up Jack gingerly.

"I will be right back," Dr. Tracy said.

"I need to call Philippe," Shawna told her mother.

"Go ahead," she said. "I'll wait here."

She went into the hall. Philippe picked up on the second ring.

"There's been an accident," Shawna said.

"What the fuck?" Philippe cried.

"He is going to be okay." Shawna said. "We're in the emergency room. My mom is here."

"What happened?" Philippe asked.

"Oh, my God, I'm so stupid!" Shawna cried. "The bath water was too hot and I forgot to test it before I put him in. I burned his legs."

"Jesus Christ," Philippe said. Shawna detected something in his tone that suggested something like this was inevitable.

"It was an accident," Shawna said.

"I should call my parents," Philippe said.

"Just come down," Shawna said. "You can call them later."

By the time Shawna hung up, Jack had fallen asleep on her shoulder. The gauze pads on his legs were oozing and the sight made her hate herself for screwing up so badly. She went back into the room where her mother was talking to an older male doctor.

"Ms. Black," the new doctor said. "As Dr. Tracy said, your baby's burns will heal with time. No scary surgery will be necessary. We would like to keep him overnight to make sure that the wounds are properly cleaned and dressed. The nurses will teach you how to change his bandages."

Vivian spoke up. "Shawna lives with me. The nurse can teach both of us."

"Were you home at the time of the accident?" the doctor asked.

"No, I teach at Berkeley," Vivian said. "Shawna called me immediately."

"So tell me what happened, Shawna," the doctor said.

"I feel so stupid." Tears sprang to her eyes. "I always test the bath water with my elbow, just like they taught us in prenatal school. Somehow, today I forgot." She omitted the part about Jack slipping out of her hand. Shawna looked at her mother. "Tell him how careful I am," she pleaded.

//

The hospital admitted Jack; Shawna and her mom accompanied his stretcher as they wheeled him up to Pediatrics on the fifth floor. Shawna sat on the bed, stroking Jack's head as he slept. Vivian claimed the lone armchair.

"You don't need to stay, Mom," Shawna said.

"Every new mom has done something like this, Shawna," her mom said. "I did it to you, my mom did it to me. Why do you think they teach you how to test the bathwater in the prenatal class? Do you think you are the first mom to burn her baby in the bath? Being a teen mom has nothing to do with it. It looks much worse than it is. The doctors know that. Although it probably helps that you are living with me and not in some rat-infested basement downtown."

"Somehow you are not making me feel any better," Shawna said. "I would rather be the first teen mom to *not* injure her baby."

"Okay, sweetie." Her mom stood and kissed Shawna on the head. "I'll see you tomorrow."

///

Shawna put Jack into the bassinet, the same type of plastic box that he was transported in when he was born. She climbed into the bed and stared at the ceiling. She was struck by the thought that it seemed like only yesterday that they were in this very same hospital and how different everything felt now. She watched Jack's blanket rise and fall with each breath and thought what a good, sweet baby he was and how was she ever going to protect him from all of her mistakes, past and future. *What have I done by bringing him into the world?*

She thought of Jack at eighteen, struggling in college like she was and feeling like shit. Having his hopes raised and shattered in work and in life—falling in love and having his heart broken. She thought about blood and accidents and death and dismemberment until a wave of grief rolled over her, smashing her onto the rock-hard hospital mattress.

//

The next morning, Mrs. Henri arrived to take them home.

"Where's Philippe?" Shawna asked. "He was supposed to come last night."

"Some school event," Mrs. Henri said. "And this morning, he has class."

"Couldn't even be bothered to visit his son in the hospital?" Shawna muttered.

"Well, I am here now so let's get you two cleaned up," Mrs. Henri said. "Your mom came by last night with a change of clothes for the baby."

Shawna changed Jack on the hospital bed, dressing him in a t-shirt and sweatshirt but leaving his legs bare. Mrs. Henri was staring at Jack's legs from across the room.

"Poor baby," Mrs. Henri said.

"I know it looks horrible," Shawna said. "But the nurse put a topical cream on it and he doesn't seem to be in any pain. Otherwise, he would be screaming."

"Stuff like this happens, Shawna," Mrs. Henri said. "Nobody is blaming you."

Yeah right, Shawna thought.

//

Shawna buckled Jack carefully into the car seat. He looked like a tiny, maimed soldier with his thick gauzy bandages. She sat in the back seat next to him and was glad she did because Mrs. Henri was a terrible driver, swerving, honking and braking madly.

"Did Philippe tell you about the time I spilled coffee on him?" Mrs. Henri shouted from the front seat. "This little episode reminded me of it. I had just purchased a new coffee maker and I was trying to figure out how to use it when the whole damn thing exploded and baby Philippe was covered from head to toe in coffee grounds and hot water. What a mess!"

"How badly was he burned?" Shawna asked. She thought about what her mom had said—*you are not the first mom to burn her baby.*

"I don't even remember," Mrs. Henri said, laughing. "I don't even think we took him to the hospital. Just tossed him in a cool bath and wiped him up. This stuff happens." She braked suddenly at a red light. Jack's head bobbled on his neck and Shawna clutched the seat back in front of her.

Twenty

SOMEHOW THEY MADE IT SAFELY HOME AND SHAWNA settled Jack in his crib. The car ride had made him drowsy and she was happy to have a few moments to herself. She logged onto Facebook.

Shawna: I burned my baby with the bath water. I'm a terrible mother!

Jasmine: Is he okay?

Shawna: We just got back from the hospital. They kept him overnight. Second-degree burns on his legs.

Aleecia: Second degree—that's bad, right?

Lucie: I googled it—some blisters, no permanent scars. WebMD says to feed him twice as much as usual.

Shawna: How do I do that?

Candy: Offer him a bottle every hour and see if he'll take it. Babies are just like dogs, they'll keep eating even after they aren't hungry.

Izzy: Dogs or people. I could eat ice cream all day.

//

"Gaby and I had lunch yesterday," Shawna's mom announced at breakfast a couple of weeks later.

Shawna was feeding Jack in his high chair, scooping applesauce and mashed peas out of little jars. His bandages were off and his burns had scabbed over.

"That's interesting," Shawna said. "I didn't know that you two were friendly."

"Not friends," she said. "But we're family now." Her mom poured herself a second cup of coffee and sat down next to Shawna. "She is concerned— we are both concerned—about Jack's safety. You are overwhelmed with school and parenting." She took a deep breath and set her cup down on the table. "She would like Jack to go live with them until he is a little older."

"That is funny, Mom," Shawna said. "Mrs. Henri and I discussed sharing custody a month or so ago and we figured your response would be, 'over my dead body!'"

"We are not talking about joint custody," she said. "We just want to make sure there are no more *accidents*." Vivian made air-quotes with her fingers.

"What?" shrieked Shawna. "Mom, you know how much I love Jack and how careful I am with him. What happened was one freak accident. You said so yourself. So did Mrs. Henri. I am not the first mom to burn her baby. Did you know that Mrs. Henri scalded Philippe with a whole pot of hot coffee when he was a baby? You said you scalded me. What are you talking about?"

"Shawna, honey, I was twenty-eight when I had you. I was already out of graduate school and teaching full-time," she said. "You know you went to that very same daycare where you drop Jack every day."

"Exactly!" Shawna said. "I grew up fine in that daycare place—and so will he. And whatever happened to your notion that you were going to raise Jack? Remember when Mr. Henri asked you if you were going to quit your job to raise him? Whatever happened to that plan?"

"Shawna, don't be silly," her mom said. "You know I'm tenured and it would be foolish for me to leave my position. And Daddy is traveling so much these days, goodness knows. Meanwhile, Gaby is home all day and she wants to take care of Jack. You can see him as much as you like but it would take a huge burden off of you, off of all of us."

"Burden?" Shawna shrieked. "What burden does Jack pose for you? You read him a book every now and then. I don't see you feeding him and changing him and cleaning up after him! After all this—you didn't want me to get an abortion, you talked Daddy into letting me keep him—now you want me to give him up?"

"Calm down, Shawna. We're not talking about adoption," her mom said. "Just guardianship."

"Guardianship?" Shawna said, forcing her voice to sound calm. "Isn't that the same thing? She would have legal right to make all decisions about his health, welfare, and education. Isn't that basically saying that I am an unfit mother, if my child needs a legal guardian?"

"The hospital may have filed a police report. I think they are required to do that for any minor that comes in with a questionable injury," her mom said. "And I think it would take a lot of pressure off of your dad,"

"Fuck, Mom! Police report, seriously? And what about Dad? What kind of pressure are we talking about? Where is he anyway? I almost never see him, anymore."

Vivian took a long sip from her mug and

weighed her words, carefully. "You are an adult now, there is no point in trying to keep secrets from you. You know your dad has never supported the idea of you having a child at your age."

Shawna's face was ashen. She nodded.

"It has been a very divisive issue between us," her mom said. "I can't tell you how many times he has asked me what I was thinking in supporting your decision to have the baby. And you know I can't tell him the truth."

"Mom," Shawna said. "Why can't you tell him? After all these years together you really believe he would hold it against you?"

"There are two things, really," she said. "First is the shame of it—I don't think he would ever look at me the same way again. And then there is the issue of deception. All these years I have kept a secret from him. When a couple goes through that—revealing a secret that they have been hiding for years—the other spouse starts to question everything—wondering what else has been hidden.

And if there were a perfect time to tell him, it would have been when we found out about your pregnancy. So there's that, too. I've held onto it for too long. He would never forgive me."

"Where is he?" Shawna asked again.

"He got an apartment in Sacramento," she said. "He has been working on a huge corruption case and the commute became too much for him. At least that's what he has told me. Maybe he has a girlfriend there. I don't know." She looked crushed, about to cry.

"Mom!" Shawna said. "You can't be serious? Dad does not have a girlfriend!"

"Well, I think if Gaby took Jack and you moved into the dorm, I might be able to coax him to come back home," she said.

"This is not my fault!" Shawna said. "I am not giving up my baby to save your marriage. This can't be happening. I'll talk to Dad."

"No, you will not!" she barked. "This is none of your business. I should not have said anything."

"I'll talk to Mrs. Henri, too," Shawna said. "I am an adult and nobody can make any custody or guardianship decisions without my consent. Nobody is taking my baby."

//

While Shawna was nursing Jack in between classes, she texted her father.

Hi, Dad. I miss you. Can we have lunch this weekend?

Dad: Sure, kiddo. Will you come here?

Shawna: Mom said you got an apartment? Can I see it?

Dad: Not really an apartment. The firm put me up at an Extended Stay hotel. It is kind of a dump, really. Lots of long distance truckers and folks like that.

Shawna: Okay. Then let's meet at a restaurant—something good for kids.

Dad: You are bringing the baby?

Shawna: Yeah. We are kind of attached at the hip.

Dad: I'll find a spot and text you.

Shawna: Coolio.

Was her Mom losing her mind? Dad didn't have an apartment in Sacramento and he certainly didn't have a girlfriend. And what was this nonsense about giving Jack to the Henris? *I will get to the bottom of this.*

Twenty One

Mrs. Henri didn't know how to do text messaging so Shawna dialed her cell.

"Hello?" Mrs. Henri answered.

"Hi, Mrs. Henri, it's Shawna."

"Shawna! How nice to hear from you. Are you calling to schedule a play date?"

"Yes, how is Sunday afternoon? Around two?" Shawna suggested.

"That would be lovely, dear. I'll have Philippe pick you up with all of the baby gear," Gaby said.

"So you haven't bought a crib or anything?" Shawna asked.

"No, why?" Mrs. Henri asked. She sounded suspicious.

"Just curious what I need to bring, that's all," Shawna said with satisfaction. "Bye." She hung up the phone.

Jack was finished nursing so she burped him and changed him and handed him back to the daycare worker.

She still had time before her next class so she logged onto Facebook.

Shawna: My mom wants me to give my baby up!

Jasmine: For adoption?

Shawna: She wants my baby-daddy's family to take custody.

Aleecia: Wait a second! I thought your mom said that SHE wanted to raise the baby!

Shawna: Yeah, well that was all bullshit. And my dad apparently left because he and my mom are fighting about the baby.

Candy: Oh, shit, my parents split up over my

baby too. Why is it that men always just want to get rid of the baby??

Luci: I had an abortion a few months ago and I can relate to many of the girls/women on here. I'm 14 years old and I've been having sex with a guy that's in his 20's. A combination of irresponsibility and plain bad luck caused the pregnancy. When we found out that I was pregnant my dad decided that I would get an abortion. I thought I would've been okay after I did it, but I've kind of been a mess ever since.

Aleecia: Jesus loves you, Luci.

Izzy: You don't have to agree to do it, do you?

Shawna: I'm going to talk to my dad this weekend.

Jasmine: Let us know what happens.

//

On Saturday, Shawna drove the eighty miles to Sacramento. Jack played happily in his car seat. He was starting to make noises that almost sounded like words. Shawna cranked up the radio and sang along with Jack interjecting, "Bah, bah, bah." Her dad had chosen to meet at a Denny's and Shawna found a spot in the parking lot. He was waiting for them at a booth in the back with a high chair.

"Daddy!" Shawna cried when she saw him. He rose and gave her a hug and kissed Jack on the head.

Shawna tucked Jack into the high chair and sat down.

"Denny's," she said. "I can't remember the last time we ate at a Denny's. I wonder if I can get breakfast?"

"They serve breakfast all day," her dad said. "Twenty-four-seven."

"Do you eat here a lot?" Shawna asked.

"No, I need to watch my waistline," he said.

"You look great, Dad," Shawna said.

"You do too, sweetie," he said. "You have really lost weight."

"Sometimes I am so tired I forget to eat," Shawna said.

The waitress approached and they ordered.

When the waitress was gone, Shawna took a big sip of ice water. "How are you, Dad?"

"This case is really big—Villalobos? The CalPERS corruption case? Have you been following it?" he asked. "The firm stands to earn millions. When this is over, I plan to take your mom to Europe."

"Oh, I am so happy to hear that!" Shawna said. And then, matter-of-factly, she blurted out, "I think Mom is worried that you are having an affair and that is why you never come home anymore."

"That is ridiculous," he exclaimed. "She comes here every other weekend!"

"Oh, I didn't realize that," Shawna said. "I thought she was traveling for work. She never said anything."

The waitress brought their food and Shawna dug into her stack of pancakes.

"Dad," Shawna paused between bites. "Mom

said that you are mad at her about me having Jack. She wants me to grant custody to Philippe and his family. She says that it is what you want?"

"She said that?" he asked.

"She said that if I give up Jack and move into a dorm that you will come back home," Shawna said.

"Where is she getting this stuff? I will be back home as soon as this phase of the case wraps up," he said. "In a month or so. She knows that. I will have to come back for phase two but that won't kick off until next year. I know it's a big sacrifice for your mom but we talked about it a lot before I took this case on. And I promised her a trip to Europe this summer. It will be like a second honeymoon. What the hell is happening?"

"So how do you really feel about Jack?" Shawna asked. "About me and Jack?"

Her father cleared his throat. "I will be honest with you. I was hurt and disappointed when you told us that you were pregnant. Disappointed in

Philippe too. We didn't know him that well but I know that you two have been friends for a few years. We had big dreams for you—college, maybe medical school or law school. Having a baby so young—that can really derail your life plans. I know that abortion is a rough experience, a tough decision—but I thought that would have been best for you."

"Did you know that mom had an abortion?" Shawna asked.

"What?" he exclaimed. All the color drained from his face.

"When she was seventeen, way before she met you," Shawna said.

"I didn't know about that," he said. He looked relieved. "And it doesn't matter. Her family probably felt the same way that we did—they wanted Vivian to go to college and achieve her dreams. And she has."

"The thing is," Shawna said. "She says she thinks about that baby every single day. Abortion isn't really the answer. You live with the guilt forever. And she blames herself for the miscarriages. She is afraid the abortion damaged her somehow so that she could never have a second child." Shawna was putting it *all* on the table.

Her father looked aghast. "She told you all of this and she has never told me?"

"She is so ashamed," Shawna said. "She made me promise I would never tell you but then she said the reason you moved out is because you are mad at her for supporting my decision to keep Jack."

"Now, she is just making shit up!" he exclaimed. "I'm sorry." He glanced guiltily at Jack.

Shawna laughed. She had rarely heard her dad swear. "Jack will learn those words soon enough, dad. He's in daycare, remember?"

"Look," her father said. "Your mom and I fought about it, sure. I was opposed to you keeping the baby and I never could fathom why she was in favor of it. But I was never going to leave her or you or Jack." He reached his hand out and Jack grabbed his thumb. "I have to talk to your mother about this," he said, pulling his phone from his pocket.

"Wait, call her later, okay? I need to talk to you about this stuff."

"Okay," he said.

Shawna continued with the pressing, straightforward questions. "So how do you feel about my decision, now?" Shawna asked.

"I think you are doing an admirable job," her dad said. "I know how hard it is—being a single mom and going to college. And your mom and I both love Jack. We love being grandparents."

"Then why is she asking me to give him up?" Shawna asked. "I just don't understand."

Twenty Two

"**N**OBODY IS ASKING YOU TO GIVE **J**ACK UP," HE SAID. "Your mother thinks that you are overwhelmed. Everyone thinks you are overwhelmed. If Gaby is able and willing to care for Jack while you finish school, is that such a bad thing? Everyone is only thinking of you and what is best for you and for Jack."

"I wish I could believe you, but Mom is acting so weird," Shawna said. "I mean, like, totally crazy. Do you think she is losing her marbles?"

"I'll be honest with you," her dad said. "I really thought so last year when she encouraged you to keep the baby and said she wanted to raise him. I didn't know where that was coming from. I guess, now I understand a little better."

"And now she's talking about you having an affair and me moving into a dorm?" Shawna added.

"I think you may be misinterpreting her words," her dad said.

Shawna saw that he was closing ranks with her mother and started to feel paranoid. Was everybody in on this? Even her Dad?

"Mrs. Henri approached me a couple of months ago about sharing custody," Shawna said. "She loves being a grandmother and Jack has had play dates at her house a few times. I sure wouldn't mind having every other weekend off when he gets a little older and he is no longer nursing. But I don't want to grant the Henris custody or guardianship. You are the lawyer, what do you think?"

"I agree with you," he said. "Giving them any kind of legal control could have long term ramifications that you can't foresee. What if Philippe eventually marries someone else and moves to another state?"

"What if Philippe marries someone else? Dad!" Shawna exclaimed. "How come nobody takes us seriously?"

"You can't predict the future," he said. "Our current agreement covers financial support and gives you complete discretion over visitation rights. I think you are doing the right thing—involving Philippe and his family, to the extent they desire. But you need to maintain legal control. I will talk to your mother about it."

"You won't tell her that I told you?" Shawna asked. "She and I are already not getting along too well. She told you about the scalding?"

"In the bathtub?" He rubbed Jack's foot. "It looks like he is healing just fine. You know every mom does that, right? Burns their kid somehow— in the bathtub, near the stove, in a hot car seat, a little too much sun at the beach, whatever. My mom did it to me; your mom did it to you."

"Mrs. Henri did it to Philippe!" Shawna laughed.

"You see!" Her dad laughed too. "Yes, I promise that your mom's secret is safe with me. I appreciate you telling me all of this, Honey. I think I'll surprise her with a visit next weekend and I'll bring flowers and maybe something sparkly. She must be feeling neglected and overwhelmed. I'm sorry she is blaming you."

"I am glad we got together. This was really nice, Dad," Shawna said.

"It was," he said. "We should do this more often. There is a pool at the hotel. Why don't we plan a play date? When are you off from school?"

"School." Shawna frowned. "About that. I am not doing too well this semester. I think I need to drop a couple of courses and cut back to part-time status. It will take me a lot longer to graduate but I'll be able to keep up with the work better."

Her dad reached across the table and took Shawna's hand. "I understand. You are trying to do too much. Cut back for now and when Jack is a little older and can stay with Gaby some days you can go back to full-time. I'm proud of you for starting classes six weeks after giving birth. I was worried that you would put it off for another semester."

Her dad paid the check and walked Shawna to her car. He buckled Jack into his car seat and leaned in through the driver's-side window for a last hug.

"Don't tell your mom that I'm coming home on Friday," he reminded her. "Let me surprise her."

///

Philippe showed up at one-thirty on Sunday and Shawna was still in her pajamas.

"C'mon!" he said. "You haven't even taken a shower yet?"

"Jack took a long nap this morning so I used the time to finish my homework," Shawna said. "I'm actually caught up this week. First time, ever!"

"Wow," Philippe said. "You seem different."

"Different, how?" Shawna asked.

"More energy?" Philippe said. "You have been acting kind of mopey lately."

"My mom said the same thing," Shawna said. "I saw my dad yesterday and we had the *best* talk! I guess I needed to know that someone's on my side."

"I am on your side," Philippe said. "Who is not on your side?"

"My mom, your mom," Shawna said. "They met this week to talk about granting custody to your family."

"Is this about the bathtub incident?" Philippe asked, incredulous. "You know . . . "

"I know! I have heard it a thousand times. Every mom burns her baby!"

"My mom dumped a whole pot of coffee on my head!" Philippe said.

"Do you remember that happening?" Shawna asked.

"No! I was just a little kid," Philippe said. "But I have heard that story so many times. And she tells it like it belongs on *America's Funniest Home Videos*!"

"I don't even think she took you to the hospital," Shawna said. "She just dumped you in a cold bath. Unbelievable." She squinted and looked closely at Philippe's forehead. "I think I can see some scars."

"Cut it out!" Philippe laughed. "Get in the shower. I'll pack up the car."

//

"Could you turn the radio down?" Shawna asked. As usual Philippe had the rap station playing full blast.

"My dad says we should stick to the current agreement which covers financial support and broad visitation rights," Shawna said. "I am happy to let your mom take Jack as often as she likes, but we are not making any legal changes."

"You sound like a lawyer," Philippe said.

"You know my dad told me for the first time yesterday that he was hoping I would go to law school," Shawna said. "I *never* knew that! My family has so many fucking secrets."

"Does my mom know that you know about the meeting with your mom?" Philippe asked.

"I'm not sure," Shawna said. "And I'm not sure whose idea it was. My mom told me some weird shit about my dad having an affair because of Jack. I think she is losing her marbles. How do we bring this up with your mom?"

Philippe gasped. "Your dad is having an affair?"

"No!" Shawna said. "She is full of shit. Even my dad said so. I told him about my mom's abortion and he was totally cool with it. My parents really don't seem to know each other at all."

"Let's just bring up the babysitting thing and see what my mom says," Philippe said. "If she doesn't bring up the custody thing, then we won't. Just pretend we don't know a thing about it. Okay?"

"Frankly, I could use the help. I don't want to start college with Cs and Ds my freshman year. I've got to pull my grades up. I am going to try to ask for some extra credit. Let's ask your mom if she would take Jack a couple of evenings this week. She could pick him up from daycare and then you could bring him back at eleven? Would that work?"

"Shawna Black getting Cs and Ds?" Philippe said. "Oh, my Lord. The sky is falling."

Shawna punched him in the arm.

"Mommy is beating me up, Jack! Help, help!" Jack kicked his feet and giggled.

Twenty Three

PHILIPPE UNLOADED THE CAR AND SET EVERYTHING UP IN the living room while Shawna changed Jack's diaper on Philippe's bed. She had never been in his room before. The room was cluttered, the dresser and closets overflowed and she felt claustrophobic. Shawna noticed that Philippe's bed took up all of the floor space; there was not enough room to fully open the dresser drawers or the closet door. The venetian blinds were heavy with dust and Shawna found herself wondering if Mrs. Henri had ever cleaned them.

David walked into the bedroom and Shawna

jumped. "Oh! Hi, Mr. Henri, I didn't know that you were home."

Mr. Henri closed the bedroom door quietly. "Shawna, I would like to have a word with you."

Shawna had never been alone with Philippe's dad before, had never spoken with him directly. "Um, sure. Let me just dump this poopy diaper. Can we talk in the living room?"

"I would like to talk in here," he said. The room was starting to get warm and the odor from the diaper was nauseating.

"It's really hot in here." Shawna started for the door and Mr. Henri stood firm in the doorway.

His voice was cold and stern when he said, "You have railroaded this family for long enough, young lady. It is time for you to take some responsibility for your actions."

Shawna was scared. "My actions?" she said. "I *am* taking responsibility for my actions. What do you mean, railroad? What are you saying?"

"You made the decision to have this child,

unilaterally. And you decided to keep this child, against the wishes of Philippe and me and the rest of his family. Your father forced us into a financial agreement against our will. Let me tell you, young lady, we are not in a position to support this child for eighteen years. What if you decide to send him to private school? Are we on the hook for that? What about college? Who will pay for his college education?"

"Can we have this conversation with Philippe in the room?" Shawna asked. *Where is this line of questioning going? Is he threatening me?*

"Philippe is a child," David said. "You have manipulated and coerced him into a situation that is out of his control."

"He seems pretty happy with the way every-thing worked out," Shawna said. "He loves Jack. I thought you loved him too."

"Your mother has rethought her position and wants to give up custody of the child," Mr. Henri said, ominously.

Shawna gasped. *My mother? Custody? What?* "My mother doesn't have custody to give up," Shawna said. "I'm the only one with legal custody. And I'm not giving it up. If you don't want to pay child support, then fine, don't. It's not your obligation. It's Philippe's."

"And there's the rub, young lady," Mr. Henri said. "Your decision has compromised my son's entire financial future. Did you think about that?"

"Don't you think Philippe should be part of this conversation?" Shawna asked again.

"My son is too young and naïve and, frankly, too stupid to understand the long-term consequences of this mistake," Mr. Henri said.

What is happening here? Shawna wondered. *Is everyone trying to abandon us—me and Jack? Fine,* she thought. *I don't need any of you. Mom, you want to throw me out of the house? Fine! Fucking Henri family—you want us to disappear and never hear from us again? Fine! I can make that happen! I don't think my dad will abandon us. And what if he did? So what? School costs me next to nothing. I will get a job; I will find a room to rent somewhere—maybe in some rat-infested basement apartment. We will be fine. Fine!*

Jack was rolling around on the bed trying to get up on his all fours.

"Excuse me," Shawna said. She handed Mr. Henri the dirty diaper. "Could you dispose of this? My son needs me."

She grabbed Jack and pushed past Mr. Henri.

///

Shawna stalked into the living room. "Philippe, we need to go!" she said.

"Go where?" Philippe asked. "We just got here."

"Well, apparently, we are not wanted—me and Jack, I mean," she said.

"Mom?" Philippe called out. "What is going on?"

Mr. and Mrs. Henri came into the living room

and settled uneasily into chairs on opposite sides of the room.

"Philippe, sit down," Mr. Henri said.

Shawna put Jack into his bouncy chair and Philippe and Shawna sat on the sofa together. Jack bounced up and down, giggling and glancing from face to face, smiling at everyone and blowing spit bubbles.

"Shawna and I just had a little conversation," Mr. Henri began.

"Yes," Shawna interjected. "And I would like to hear from each individual in this room as to what level of involvement you would like to have in Jack's life. Mr. Henri has made it clear that he wants no financial involvement. That is perfectly fine with me. He is Jack's grandfather, not his father."

Philippe glared at his father. "What the fuck?" he mouthed.

"Mrs. Henri, we were under the impression that you would like to have visitation rights," Shawna said. "If that is not the case that is fine as well. We can walk out the door right this second and you will never see us or hear from us again. I am never giving up my baby. I just want that to be clear to everyone." Shawna was starting to feel like a prosecuting attorney.

Gaby glanced nervously at her husband who was glowering at the floor and then steeled herself. "I would like to continue to see my grandson every week," she said.

"Would you be willing to pick him up from daycare and babysit him a couple of evenings each week?" Philippe asked. "I will drive him home at the end of the night."

"Thank you," Shawna said under her breath. She was relieved that she didn't have to ask that question.

"I would love that," Mrs. Henri said. "I want to be in his life. I want Jack to know his Grandma."

"So do I," Shawna said. She felt herself begin to tear up but she took a deep breath to stem the flow. "Philippe, I have to ask you, too," Shawna said. "Your father is under the impression that I railroaded you into this situation. Is that the way you feel? Do you want to walk away from us and waive all of your parental rights and responsibilities?"

Philippe's face registered shock. "What the fuck, Dad?" he shouted. "I never said that!" He looked at Shawna and took her hand. He took a minute to gather his thoughts. "I think you are awesome, Shawna Black. You are an awesome woman and an awesome mother. And you know that we have an awesome baby! I have loved you since the moment I met you—the stupid fire drill—remember?"

Shawna blushed and laughed, "I remember," she said.

"I want to marry you, Shawna Black," Philippe said. "Just like we had always planned. Our plan was to finish college and get married and have . . . whoops, okay we got that a little bit out of order."

He laughed. "But, it does not change the way I feel about you or where I see us going in the future."

Shawna squeezed his hand as tears stung her eyes. She swallowed hard. Her voice cracked as she said, "So Mr. Henri, it seems like you are the only person in this room who wants to have no involvement with Jack. That is very sad, and I am sorry for your loss. Eventually your grandson will notice the gap in his life. But, I am fine with your decision. We do not need your money."

Mr. Henri had a look of sheer hatred on his face as he spat out his words. "I will not be shamed by you. We will meet our financial obligations." He got up and stalked out of the room.

"I am so sorry, Shawna," Mrs. Henri said. "To be honest, it was all your mom's idea. We thought you and she were on the same page."

"I know," Shawna said. "I'm sorry for being rude to your husband, Mrs. Henri. Can we leave Jack here for a couple of hours?"

Twenty Four

PHILIPPE PUT THE CAR INTO GEAR. "WOW," HE EXCLAIMED. "That was rough! What the hell happened back there?"

"Your dad accosted me in your bedroom when I was changing Jack," Shawna said. "He wouldn't let me out of the room. He blocked the door."

"Jesus," Philippe said. "He did that?"

"He scared the shit out of me," Shawna said. "And I think that was his goal. He threatened me and tried to browbeat me into giving up custody. I think he was planning to put Jack up for adoption, can you believe it?"

"He couldn't do that!" Philippe said.

"No, I don't think he could," Shawna said. "Not without your consent, anyway. I'll ask my dad about it. Basically, your dad threatened to pull all financial support and I am assuming that is what my mom wants to do, too. Throw us out on the street. I started thinking about what that would look like. I would never give up my baby, even if they tried to starve me out. My mom wants me to move into a dorm. Maybe I should apply for student family housing and live on campus. Jack and I could live in a studio apartment. My dad won't abandon us and now I know for sure, you won't either. And your mom could help with babysitting so I can keep up with my schoolwork. We can make this work even if it's only the four of us: you, me, my dad and your mom. Fuck the others!"

"Yeah, fuck them!" Philippe said. "Shit, I wonder if my dad will threaten to stop paying my tuition?"

"No, why would he do that?" Shawna said.

"He's worried about your future—he thinks I am the impediment."

Philippe pulled into Shawna's driveway. She leaned over and kissed him. "What time will you bring him back?"

"I don't know, four or five? I'll text you."

"Great." She started to get out of the car.

"Hey, Shawna," Philippe said. "You didn't say anything. What do you think about what I said back there?"

"Was that your idea of a proposal?" she smiled.

"Yes," he smiled back. "So will you?"

She smiled at him. "Yes," she said. "Yes, Philippe Henri, I will marry you."

He grinned. "Well, then, how do you feel about premarital sex?"

Shawna laughed. "I would love that," Shawna said. "I'll make an appointment with the school clinic to get an IUD first. No more screw-ups!"

//

Shawna stormed through the door. "Mom! Mom, are you home?"

Her mom was in the kitchen, flipping through a cookbook. Her face was flushed. "Your dad called," she said. "He's coming next weekend instead of me going there. How nice. I want to plan a nice dinner."

"I think he is planning to take you out for dinner," Shawna said.

"What? You knew about this?" her mom asked.

"We met for lunch yesterday," Shawna said. "Why didn't you tell me you were going to Sacramento every other weekend? You know Dad's not having an affair, too. Why did you say all that shit?"

"Watch your mouth," her mom said sharply.

"Sorry, Mom," Shawna said. "Why did you tell me that?"

"He has been gone so long," her mom said. "We had a big fight about you and Jack and then the next thing I hear is that he is staying in Sacramento over the weekend and then one weekend led to two. And now it has been going on for months. You know how a woman's mind works."

"But you have been seeing him every other weekend?" Shawna said.

"I know but it's not the same thing as waking up next to your husband every morning," her mom said. "We can go for days without talking at all."

"Okay. I get it," Shawna said. "By the way, Philippe and I are getting married!"

"What?" her mom exclaimed. "When?"

"Oh, I don't know," Shawna said. "Some day when we both have graduated from college and have jobs and can afford our own place. Mom, can we sit down? I need to talk to you about something."

Her mom's face, flushed just moments before, was devoid of all color. "Sure," she said. They sat in the breakfast nook where Shawna imagined her parents sitting together the night before Jack's birth.

"I need to know what is going on with you and your feelings about me and Jack," Shawna said. "I talked to Dad and he is totally on board. Sure, he had reservations about the pregnancy at first, but he is one hundred percent supportive of me finishing college, and maybe even going to law school. We had such a great talk yesterday. It really helps me to know that I have his support. I would like to know that I have your support too."

"I'm glad you cleared the air with your dad," her mom said. "I really didn't know where his head was at, either. Like I said, our last conversation about you turned into a huge fight and then he stormed out. We left it at that. When I saw him on the weekends, I tried to avoid talking about you and the baby because I didn't want to stir things up."

"Okay. That helps a little," Shawna said. "When we dropped Jack at Philippe's house today, Mr. Henri accosted me."

"He what?" her mom repeated.

"He accused me of *railroading* them," Shawna

made air quotes with her fingers. "Like we forced Philippe and his family into the financial contract. Remember the *garden party*?" More air quotes.

"And then what happened?" her mom asked.

"We had a huge come-to-Jesus moment," Shawna said. "We all sat in the living room and I told them I was willing to tear up the contract and make it on my own—just me and Jack. I went around the room and asked each one what kind of involvement they wanted in Jack's life. I didn't think Mrs. Henri wanted us to cut her out and I was right. She wants to be a part of Jack's life. Forever. And she wants to start babysitting two nights a week, which will be a huge help for me in keeping up with my schoolwork. Then I asked Philippe what he wanted and that's when he said—right in front of his parents—that he wants to marry me."

"What did David say?" her mom asked.

"Well at that point, he was too ashamed to say, *Fuck off, Shawna*, right in front of everyone. He actually said, and I quote: 'We will meet our financial obligations.' And then he stormed out. He was acting really scary."

"Wow," her mom said. "You are one brave girl—woman, I mean."

"So, Mom," Shawna said. "What is your answer? What level of involvement would you like to have in Jack's life: financial, emotional, caregiving-wise? I have to tell you, I got the distinct impression from our last conversation that you want us out of here. You wanted me to give away my child and move into a dorm. Isn't that what you said? Do you realize that Mr. Henri would have given Jack up for adoption? Or he would have tried. Philippe would never have agreed to it, thank God."

With this comment hanging in the air, Vivian started to weep. "I'm sorry, Shawna. I only said that because I thought your dad was leaving me. I thought if I could turn back the clock to before this had all happened, if I had agreed with him that you should get an abortion, he would never have moved to Sacramento. It was magical thinking."

"Mom," Shawna said, gently. "I am pretty sure, if you hadn't started going to see him in Sacramento, he would have been home every weekend. I think to him, it was kind of romantic for you two to have a little getaway every other weekend. You are acting paranoid and, frankly, psycho."

"You know, you are right as usual," her mom said, wiping her eyes, and managing a snort-like laugh. "It is really romantic when we are there together. No household chores, no crying baby." She started to laugh.

"He also told me he's taking you to Europe this summer, for a second honeymoon," Shawna said.

"He said second honeymoon?" Her eyes widened in amazement. "He used those words?"

"He did," Shawna said. "He also said that he felt bad that he's been neglecting you. I don't want to spoil his fun but you should expect a little surprise from him next weekend."

"Oh, wow," her mom said. "I have goose bumps. Who knew that after almost twenty years of marriage, we could still give each other goose bumps?"

"That's all great, but you didn't answer my question," Shawna said.

"Involvement in Jack's life?" her mom asked. "I want to see him every day. Believe me when I say, I did *not* know that David was planning to give Jack up. I thought we would all stay involved but Jack would live with them until you finished school. That is all that Gaby and I discussed." She took Shawna's hand. "I want to help you however I can, with financial and emotional support."

"Do you think you could commit to babysitting two nights a week?" Shawna said. "One weeknight so I can focus on my schoolwork and one weekend night so I could have date night with my fiancé?"

"I could do one weeknight, sure, but every weekend—that's a lot, honey. Maybe I could watch him one night every *other* weekend?" her mom asked. "When I'm not in Sacramento?"

"Dad said he is coming home in a month," Shawna said. "The first phase of his case is almost wrapped up."

"Okay. When your dad gets home," her mom said, "we'll up it to every weekend."

"Thanks, Mom." Shawna gave her mother a hug.

Twenty Five

SHAWNA WALKED OUT TO THE BACK PATIO, THE SCENE of the "garden party." She collapsed onto the chaise, stared at the clouds in the bright blue sky, and reflected on the events of the past year. She almost didn't recognize the girl who had seriously contemplated aborting her child. Everyone had told her that it was the easiest, the best, solution. That she would be able to forget that she had ever gotten pregnant and go on with her life—college, career. *The choice my mom had made,* she thought. *Where would that child be now—my older brother or sister? My mom must be asking herself that, every day. Well, I'm glad I'll never have to.*

The future suddenly looked less bleak, more manageable. She remembered her mother's words: "it takes a village." Shawna had negotiated childcare commitments from Mrs. Henri and her mom, secured financial support from Mr. Henri. And Philippe had asked her to marry him. Now it was her turn—no more excuses. She would have to work harder at keeping up with her schoolwork. She was more determined than ever to pull up her grades. *Maybe I'll even apply to law school. It would be exciting to be a criminal defense attorney like my dad!*

"We can do this, Jack," she said out loud. *I hope you can feel my love for you right now. You are one beloved little boy and you brought us all together—Dad and Mom. And Philippe and me. And Grandma Gaby. And I have a feeling that even Grandpa David will come around, eventually. I'll bet you that he will show up for your soccer matches, your swim meets, and your piano recitals. But no football games. I don't want you playing football.*

Oh, and sorry again about the scalding. Apparently every mom burns their baby. One day, we'll laugh about it.